"Commander, this is Worf!" the young Klingon responded.

"Instrumentation indicates we have a Level One intrusion. A ship classified as belonging to a hostile species is within our defense perimeter!"

"Identify!" replied Commander Clark.

Soleta was already on it. She studied the readings and called out, "Configuration indicates a Romulan vessel, closing fast."

"I'm alerting Starfleet," said Clark. "Keep feeding me readings. Clark to Level Five. Tobias and Briggs, prepare defensive weaponry—"

"They're not cloaked!" yelled McHenry. "Why aren't they cloaked?"

"Logically," said Soleta with amazing calm, "they decloak when they are preparing to—"

Prometheus Station rocked around them, knocking all of them off their feet. Worf crashed to the ground, Soleta tumbling down atop him. Over the explosions and the shouts, they heard Clark yelling over the comm units. Telling the cadets not to panic, telling them to do their jobs. . . .

THE NEXT GENERATION™

STARFLEET ACADEMY™#1
WORF'S FIRST
ADVENTURE

Peter David

A
MINSTREL®
BOOK

PUBLISHED BY POCKET BOOKS

New York   London   Toronto   Sydney   Tokyo   Singapore

A MINSTREL PAPERBACK *ORIGINAL*

A Minstrel Book published by
POCKET BOOKS, a division of Simon & Schuster Inc.
1230 Avenue of the Americas, New York, NY 10020

Copyright © 1993 by Paramount Pictures. All rights reserved.

STAR TREK is a Registered Trademark of
Paramount Pictures.

This book is published by Pocket Books, a division of
Simon & Schuster Inc., under exclusive license from
Paramount Pictures.

ISBN: 0-671-87084-X

First Minstrel Books printing August 1993

10 9 8 7 6 5 4 3 2 1

A MINSTREL BOOK and colophon are registered trademarks of
Simon & Schuster Inc.

Cover art by Catherine Huerta

Printed in the U.S.A.

Dedicated to Next Generations everywhere

STARFLEET TIMELINE

2264

The launch of Captain James T. Kirk's five-year mission, _U.S.S. Enterprise,_ NCC-1701.

2292

Alliance between the Klingon Empire and the Romulan Star Empire collapses.

2293

Colonel Worf, grandfather of Worf Rozhenko, defends Captain Kirk and Doctor McCoy at their trial for the murder of Klingon chancellor Gorkon.

Khitomer Peace Conference, Klingon Empire/Federation (_Star Trek VI_).

2323

Jean-Luc Picard enters Starfleet Academy's standard four-year program.

2328

The Cardassian Empire annexes the Bajoran homeworld.

2341

Data enters Starfleet Academy.

2342

Beverly Crusher (née Howard) enters Starfleet Academy Medical School, an eight-year program.

2346

Romulan massacre of Klingon outpost on Khitomer.

2351

In orbit around Bajor, the Cardassians construct a space station
that they will later abandon.

2353

William T. Riker and Geordi La Forge enter Starfleet Academy.

2354

Deanna Troi enters Starfleet Academy.

2356

Tasha Yar enters Starfleet Academy.

2357

Worf Rozhenko enters Starfleet Academy.

2363

Captain Jean-Luc Picard assumes command of U.S.S. Enterprise, NCC-1701-D.

2367

Wesley Crusher enters Starfleet Academy.
An uneasy truce is signed between the Cardassians and the Federation.
Borg attack at Wolf 359; First Officer Lieutenant Commander
Benjamin Sisko and his son, Jake, are among the survivors.
U.S.S. Enterprise-D defeats the Borg vessel in orbit around Earth.

2369

Commander Benjamin Sisko assumes command of Deep Space
Nine in orbit over Bajor.

Source: Star Trek® Chronology / Michael Okuda and Denise Okuda

CHAPTER

1

The young Klingon saw it before anyone else.

He squinted against the sun for a moment while his brother was still deep in conversation with their parents. Then he stabbed a finger in the air and said, "There!"

The three humans turned to see where he was indicating. "Where?" said the father. "I don't . . . no, wait! He's right! There it comes!"

The shuttle transport dropped gracefully from the sky, actually seeming to flutter over the Russian landscape like a feather in the breeze. Now that it was in view, it approached with startling speed. One moment it was no larger than a penny against the sun, and the next, it was cruising directly overhead, angling down toward the landing pad some yards away. Technicians were already scrambling to meet and service the vehicle, prepping it for the continuation of its voyage.

Young Worf Rozhenko turned to face his parents. They were so beaming with pride that, if they had been suns, he would have been blinded by the light. What was the word he'd heard his foster mother use? *K'velling*. It sounded vaguely Klingonese, but his mother insisted it was some ancient tongue called Yiddish.

Sergey Rozhenko, his adopted father, was a robust barrel-chested man. His hair and beard were showing the first serious signs of graying. At first Sergey had refused to believe the alteration in the coloring of his hair, claiming loudly—and repeatedly—that no Rozhenko male had ever gone gray. Then, one day, Worf had simply pointed out that no Rozhenko male had ever had to deal with raising a young Klingon. This caused five minutes of hysterical laughter from both his parents. He would never forget Sergey Rozhenko, slapping his knee and pointing and saying, "You're right, Worf! You're absolutely right! If every Rozhenko father had to deal with a Klingon son, we'd be gray by thirty and bald by forty!"

His father was a strong man, both physically and temperamentally. His mother, Helena, was just as strong, but in a different way. Where Sergey was boisterous, Helena was reserved. Where Sergey was demanding, Helena was persuasive. They complemented each other perfectly and between the two of them could accomplish just about anything.

Next to Worf stood his brother, Simon. Worf did not need to guess what his father had looked like when he was a young man. Simon was the image of him. He was beardless, revealing the strong jawline that their father's facial growth hid. But he had the same black hair, the same ready smile, and the same confident, gleaming eyes. The only real difference was that he had the smaller, more delicate nose of Helena, which almost looked like something of a mismatch in the otherwise rugged face. Sergey loudly proclaimed that sooner or later the boy would be in a good, solid brawl, get his nose broken, and look just like his father . . . a notion about which Helena was not particularly enthusiastic.

Technically, Worf should have been thinking of Simon as his adopted brother. But never, in all the years that they had been together—and Worf had difficulty remembering now a time when they hadn't been—Simon had never done anything to make Worf feel as if he were anything less than a full-fledged, full-blooded member of the Rozhenko family. Nor had Sergey and Helena Rozhenko themselves.

And yet . . .

There had been those others.

Worf's scowl deepened in that way that his mother had come to recognize instantly. Her first, emotional response was to embrace her Klingon son. Crush him to her, assure him that everything was going to be better now. That the public school taunts Worf had endured throughout his childhood and into his teens would be a thing of the past.

But she knew him too well. She knew that such words of encouragement were not what he wanted to hear. All those times when he had come home after having been in yet another fight, he had not wanted, or desired, consolation.

"It is not appropriate, Mother," he had said to her so often that she knew every word by heart. "A warrior endures pain without complaint. Nothing less is to be expected."

"But you're not a warrior!" she had once replied in frustration. "You're a boy, nowhere near grown! And you're hurting, even if you don't want to admit it! Don't shut me out, Worf!"

But he had.

Because he was Klingon, and that was simply the way things were.

It had taken her a long time to come to terms with that. She had finally managed to, though . . . or, at least, she thought she had.

Still, when she saw her son, Simon, embracing his father—hugging the older man with such strength that it seemed as if he might snap him in half—just for a moment she wanted to fold Worf into her arms. Hold her adopted Klingon son one more time before he went off to Starfleet Academy to become a man.

But she held herself back. Instead, drawing herself up stiffly, she extended a hand.

"Good luck, Worf," she said.

Just for a moment she was certain that she saw a fleeting look of gratitude in his eyes. An emotional display, while being very fulfilling for her, would have been tremendously embarrassing for him. He took the hand and shook it firmly. "Thank you, Mother."

Unable to help herself, she added, "Don't let your hair grow too long. We're always arguing about that."

Worf made a "harrumph" noise. "A true Klingon warrior's hair is long . . . and preferably uncombed."

His father glanced at him, relaxing his embrace on Simon. "If you're in the Klingon Empire," he said firmly, "you can be as unkempt as you like. But," he rumbled, "when you're in Starfleet, you'll abide by the codes of appearance. You understand that, don't you, Worf."

The phrasing was not a question, and clearly only one answer was acceptable. "Yes, Father," replied Worf.

It was a bit easier for his father to resist hugging him. His father had once been in Starfleet, and formality on special occasions came naturally to him. He shook Worf's hand firmly, and even managed not to wince at the strength of the boy's grip.

The shuttlecraft had landed, and technicians were getting flight updates from the pilot. Through one of the shuttle windows, Worf caught a glimpse of a young woman with pointed ears and upswept eyebrows. Unmistakably she was a Vulcan, and Worf felt a brief rush of excitement. He'd never seen one before. And now he'd be attending class at Starfleet Academy with one!

There was someone else at another window, and this individual drew a frown from Worf. It was a human boy with short-cropped red hair. For reasons that Worf could not guess, the youth was staring intently at the window, touching the tip of his nose with his finger. He would then bring his finger slowly to the window, touch the window . . . and then return it to his nose. As Worf watched, the young man did it three times, apparently oblivious to the oddness of his behavior.

Mentally, Worf shrugged. Who could understand the mysteries of humans? He had lived among them for almost as long as he could remember, first on the farming planet of Gault, and then on Earth, in Russia, since he was eleven years of age. The time spent with his Klingon parents on the now destroyed colony of Khitomer seemed, more and more frequently, a mere dream that was fading fast. A dream that he often had to fight to hold on to.

There was nothing more to say. He nodded formally to his parents, picked up his bag, and headed for the shuttle.

Simon started to follow, but Helena put a hand on his shoulder.

In a low voice she said, "Watch out for your brother, Simon. Make certain he's all right."

"Of course, Mother," he said, sounding a bit puzzled. "But Worf has always been rather self-sufficient, don't you think? He doesn't need a babysitter."

"No. But he does need support. He needs to know that

he has someone to turn to. Even strong people need to draw strength from those around them. Be there for him to lean on, Simon." She kissed him on the cheek. "I'm counting on you."

"Don't worry so, Helena!" Sergey boomed in his most confident voice. "The Rozhenko brothers, together at Starfleet Academy! What possible obstacle could arise that they would not be able to handle, eh?"

Simon smiled readily, as he so often did. "Nothing, Father," he said.

But as he headed toward the shuttlecraft, he felt the first pang of unease. He glanced back to see his parents waving, and his father giving him a confident thumbs-up.

He hoped that he could remain as confident as his father.

There were two empty seats on the shuttle. Worf took the one toward the back. It was reflex. Worf had long ago gotten into the habit of sitting at the farthest point from the door in any room—preferably with his back against a wall. This made it impossible for anyone to sneak up and attack him from behind. The fact that there was little likelihood that he would be ambushed on a low-orbit shuttlecraft made no difference. Habit was habit.

The seat put him directly across the aisle from the young Vulcan woman he had glimpsed earlier. She was rather intriguing-looking. In addition to the exotic aspect of her ears and eyebrows, her black longish hair was tied back in a tail and held there by an odd, triangular-shaped gold barrette. Worf was caught by its gleam and stared at it rather openly.

Simon, for his part, was seated opposite the oddball

with the window fixation. He had ceased his strange window-to-nose-and-back ritual. Instead, he brought his mouth right up to the window, opened wide, and puffed on it, creating a small circle of moisture that misted the window over. He then began to etch some sort of numbers and equations in it, all with a very distracted air.

The shuttlecraft door closed with a *thud*. Moments after running some last-minute safety checks, the craft lifted into the air.

It angled around, and Worf—peering through his own window—was able to spot his parents. They were standing exactly where they had been before. They were still waving, as if they were windup mechanical dolls. From this height he doubted they could see him . . . and, for all they knew, he could not see them. But somehow, it clearly didn't matter to them.

They would probably stand there and wave until their arms fell off, and it didn't matter. He had a feeling that they would continue to wave until the shuttlecraft was long, long out of sight . . . and perhaps even for a few moments after that. As if waving would put off, for a little while longer, the inevitability of being left alone after nearly two decades of raising children.

He sighed for a moment and then turned his silent attention back to the Vulcan woman. She appeared intent on some text that she was reading. He glanced over at it and saw that it was in a language he didn't recognize, probably Vulcan. So he went back to studying the odd clip in her hair.

Without looking up she said, "It's an IDIC."

He blinked in surprise. "What?"

"The symbol holding my hair back. It's called an

IDIC." For the first time she looked up at him, fixing him with her dark eyes. "That is what you're staring at, correct?"

"Yes," he said, shifting a bit uncomfortably in his seat. "I . . . did not mean to embarrass you."

"Embarrass?" She stared at him as if he'd just spoken a word in some bizarre foreign tongue. "I do not 'embarrass.' It is understandable that you know nothing of the IDIC. But do you know nothing of Vulcans at all?"

"I know of Vulcans," said Worf stiffly. "You are said to prize logic above all else. To be very disciplined and totally without emotion."

"Not precisely," she said. "If we were truly without emotion, no discipline would be required. We control our emotions so that they do not interfere with other pursuits. Logic is of paramount importance. It is all we need."

"Really?" Worf was not remotely convinced. "What does your logic tell you of me, then?"

She did not hesitate. "Your parents were killed while you were young. You were adopted by a Starfleet officer, raised on a farming planet, then on Earth, and now you and your adopted brother are on your way to Starfleet Academy."

Worf's jaw dropped in amazement. "How . . . did you know all that?"

She tapped the data padd she'd been studying. "I've memorized the specifics on all incoming cadets. Since there is only one Klingon listed, and since this shuttle is bound for the Academy, logic dictates that you are Worf Rozhenko. That would be Simon?" She pointed in the direction of Worf's brother.

"Yes."

"Ah."

They regarded each other for a moment, and then Worf said, "What is an IDIC?"

"A Vulcan term," she said. "A philosophy of spiritual oneness. The actual Vulcan word is pronounced more along the lines of 'Eee-deek.' Humans have transliterated it into I-D-I-C, claiming that it stands for 'Infinite Diversity in Infinite Combination.' A convenient mnemonic memory device . . . simplistic but fairly accurate."

"What is your name?"

She raised an eyebrow. "Is that of interest to you?"

He shrugged.

"Soleta," she told him. "Now, if you will excuse me . . ."

She went back to her padd, and Worf quickly realized that she saw no "logical" reason to continue the conversation.

He glanced out the window. They had reached the upper atmosphere, the Earth spinning below them. By attaining such a high altitude, they would be able to use Earth's rotation to bring them to their destination that much faster. He called up to the shuttle pilot, "Is it permissible to stand up?"

"Stand up, walk around . . . do handstands, if you want," said the pilot. "But in ten minutes I want you buckled back up for landing."

Worf nodded acknowledgment, then got up out of his seat and moved next to where Simon was seated. Simon was still staring in fascination at the redheaded boy.

"What is he doing?" Worf asked Simon in a low voice.

Simon shook his head. "No clue. You ask him."

Undaunted, Worf reached over and tapped the boy's shoulder. "You," he said, without polite preamble. "What are you doing?"

The redhead looked at him. "When?"

"Just now."

"Talking to you."

Worf's eyes narrowed suspiciously. His first inclination was to suspect that the lad was trying to antagonize him. But he was staring at Worf with such a deadpan expression that it was impossible to tell.

"I meant before. When you were touching your nose and the window. And drawing numbers on the window."

"Oh . . . that. Abstract thinking. Thinking things. Spatial coordinates. Relations. Paradox. The halving one."

"Halving one?" Worf was beginning to feel utterly lost.

"Let's say you have a distance to travel in a straight line on a single plane," said the redhead. He had such a strange look in his eyes that Worf expected the twin orbs to begin rotating in opposite directions from each other just about any time. "From point A to point B. And you travel half the distance. And then you travel half the remaining distance. And then half of that remaining distance, and so on and so on . . . then what?"

"Then what what?" Simon asked from behind Worf.

"You'd never get there," said the redhead. "You'd just keep covering smaller and smaller distances. Why? A paradox. A question with no answer. Well . . . not all questions without answers are paradoxes. Like . . . what rhymes with orange? There's no answer to that. But that's not a paradox. That's just an annoying question. Do you like oranges?"

He stared at them intently, as if he'd just posed a question of life-and-death importance. Worf and Simon slowly nodded.

He raised a finger and said thoughtfully, "If a tree fell in a forest, and no one were around . . . then who would care?"

Worf opened his mouth to answer, and then closed it again. Simon seemed likewise stumped.

"You know what I think?" continued the redhead, apparently not caring if he got an answer to any of his previous questions . . . or even forgetting them completely. "I think there's something strange that the opposite of anti-matter isn't pro-matter. I think that should be changed, for clarity's sake."

"Who *are* you?" asked Worf in confusion.

"Mark McHenry," he said. "Who are you?"

"Simon and Worf Rozhenko," said Simon.

"Which one is which?"

"Uhhh . . . I'm Simon. That's Worf," Simon told him. Once again he and Worf exchanged looks.

"I am surprised you could not guess," said Worf dryly. "One human name, one Klingon name. It should be fairly easy to tell us apart."

"You have a Klingon name?" said McHenry. "Why?"

Simon had to stifle a laugh. For a moment Worf started to think that perhaps, as some sort of practical joke, Simon had put McHenry up to this. "Because I am a Klingon!"

McHenry's eyes focused on Worf, as if truly seeing him for the first time.

"Oh, yeah," he said. "How long have you been a Klingon?"

"Buckle up!" called the pilot, sparing Worf the necessity of addressing the odd question.

Worf retreated quickly to his seat. McHenry tossed off a wave, and then stared at the empty air for several moments before starting to pluck at the air. Simon watched for a short time and then couldn't stand it anymore. "What are you doing?"

"Trying to catch molecules," replied McHenry.

"But you can't *see* molecules!" Simon told him.

"I know. That way I never have to worry that I might have missed," he said, grabbing at the air.

Simon, wisely, said nothing more.

CHAPTER 2

The shuttlecraft made a low pass over the Golden Gate Bridge and moments later angled down to the official landing pad of Starfleet Academy.

Worf's face was pressed against the window, gaping. He had heard for so long his father's descriptions of the several buildings that made up the Academy—a fabulous combination of elegance and simplicity. It gleamed white against the noonday sun, looking as pristine and new as if it had been erected that very day instead of decades earlier.

He glanced at his classmates. Soleta barely gave the Academy a glance, but she did give a quick nod of approval. McHenry, for his part, didn't even seem to notice it. He was suddenly very intent on studying the whorls on his fingertips.

And Simon . . .

For a moment Worf thought that Simon looked a little nervous. But the thought was ridiculous, of course. Simon's whole life had prepared him for this moment. He was the best, the brightest that the Rozhenko family had to offer. Indeed, Worf had already mentally steeled himself for living in the shadow of his brother's sure-to-be-brilliant career.

Worf would simply do the best he could, and that would have to be enough.

The shuttle landed smoothly, and moments later Worf was the first to emerge from the craft. Nearby he saw other shuttlecrafts that had landed, disgorging their passengers out onto the grounds that had been trod by such Starfleet legends as Robert April, Matt Decker, James Kirk, and Rachel Garrett.

The air was much warmer here in San Francisco. Worf breathed in deeply, but it seemed insubstantial somehow. As if the local atmosphere had no character. He was long accustomed to the biting sting that Russian air seemed to carry with it.

And then, off to his left, he heard a curse.

The words were not familiar, but the tone most definitely was. Moreover, he was quite certain that it had been directed at him.

Slowly he turned his great head and found himself eye to eye with a Brikar.

As was the case with all of his race, the Brikar had no hair anywhere on his body. As was the custom when in casual dress, the Brikar was barefoot. He wore pants that were of a shiny black material . . . some sort of animal hide, Worf suspected. He also wore a black tunic that hung open. His arms were powerful and muscled. He was tridigital, his hands ending in three long fingers: two in a V-shape accompanied by an opposable thumb. In contrast to the rest of his rugged appearance, the hands looked relatively delicate. This, however, was deceptive, for they were as powerful as the rest of him.

His skin was dusky brown, with highlights of pure ebony. The actual surface of his skin was rocklike, substantiating the renowned Brikarian durability. Nowhere was this more evident than in the shape and style of his skull. It looked squared, many-faceted like a rough diamond. His ears were small holes in the sides of his head, and his nose was two vertical, parallel slits that started between his eyes and ran to just above his mouth.

His eyes were black and glittered with contempt. It was clear that he was a new arrival, since his bundle was at his feet.

"So," he said slowly, in that deliberate way that all Brikar had. "The rumors were true. A Klingon in our midst."

Worf was about to bite off a sharp reply, but then he saw Simon making a calming gesture. *Go slow. Don't let anyone bait you. This isn't grammar school anymore,* he seemed to be saying.

"That . . . is correct," Worf replied after a moment.

The Brikar's face twisted in undisguised disgust. "It's just my luck," he said. "I finally make it to the Academy, and now . . . *now* . . . is when they decide to toss admission requirements out the window and let anyone in."

Worf's fellow passengers had now emerged from the shuttle. Other students, overhearing the exchange, were drifting in their direction. Worf was feeling extremely uncomfortable at that moment.

Usually when Worf felt uncomfortable, he vented that

feeling by hitting something . . . usually an inanimate object. But there was nothing else around, and the Brikar was beginning to look awfully tempting. That, however, was no way to make a first impression.

Soleta, observing the exchange the way a scientist would watch a cell splitting, said, "I am unaware of any lessening of requirements for attendance, Brikar. However, were there any such . . . it might explain the presence of excessively belligerent individuals. Yourself, perhaps?"

The Brikar cast her a furious glance that did not disturb the young Vulcan woman in the slightest. "This isn't your affair, Vulcan," he snapped. "I have no quarrel with you."

Now Simon stepped in. "And you have none with Worf, either," he said firmly. "Worf, let's go."

Simon took his brother firmly by the arm, and at first Worf allowed himself to be led away.

But the Brikar was not about to let it slide. He followed them and said, "How appropriate. The Klingon dog, allowing himself to be led around. All you need is a leash."

Worf shook Simon loose and turned to face the Brikar. "And all you need is a muzzle," he snapped.

Now more cadets were clustering around, aware that something was going on. But now Worf took no notice of them. "What is your problem, anyway, Brikar?" he demanded.

"My problem," shot back the Brikar, "is that all Klingons know how to do is invade. To attack. To grab territory. To insert themselves where no one wants them. If the Klingons hadn't come crawling to the Federation fifty years ago—"

"We did not *crawl!*" said Worf, fury boiling over.

"You did!" said the Brikar. "Came crawling for help and started a peace initiative . . . and then, when you were back on your feet, you thought nothing of stabbing the Federation in the back—"

"It was *not* like that!" Worf snarled through gritted teeth.

"Worf, calm down!" shouted Simon. He tried to pull on Worf's arm again, but the Klingon's strength was far superior, and this time Worf wasn't allowing himself to be led away.

The Brikar was relentless. "It was exactly like that! Federation allies where it suits your purposes; enemies when you want something. Taking over planets, intruding yourselves where nobody wants you—"

"I am as entitled to be here as you are!"

"Only because no one in Starfleet was smart enough to say no!"

No one was certain who threw the first punch, including Worf and the Brikar. One moment, they were arguing, their shouting faces mere inches away from each other. And the next moment they had slammed into each other, wrestling, shoving, and grabbing. Worf landed on top, and he brought his fist back and punched the Brikar as hard as he could.

It was like hitting granite. Worf fought down the reflex to yelp in pain. In fact, he hit the Brikar again, as hard as he could, and hoped that the result wasn't going to be that he broke his own fingers.

The blow was not without effect. For a moment the Brikar seemed dazed, but then he rallied and struck back. Worf practically flew backward and hit the ground. Now the Brikar was up and charging, but he moved slower than

Worf, who twisted out of his way, avoiding the attack. His legs speared out, snagging the Brikar by the ankles, and the larger cadet went down. Worf lunged at him and they rolled, over and over, struggling and shouting at each other.

Simon tried to make himself heard over the noise, but he was not at all successful. The other cadets were bellowing far too loudly and drowning him out. "Worf, for crying out loud—!" he called, but his voice was merely one of many lost in the chaos.

The security guards, however, were able to make themselves heard with extreme ease.

They shoved their way through the collected cadets. "What the blazes is going on here!" the foremost guard was calling. They had their phasers out, ready for anything. Nevertheless, they were not entirely prepared for the sight of two would-be Starfleet cadets—one Brikar, one Klingon—pounding on each other on the grounds of the Academy.

The other cadets turned away as if suddenly concerned that their mere presence might be enough to get them thrown out of the Academy before they'd even had a chance to start.

The guards surrounded the combatants and pulled them apart. It was no easy feat, because, pound for pound, both Worf and his opponent were capable of giving a good fight to any of the guards. But the two of them were drastically outnumbered. And besides that, being surrounded by a small sea of red security uniforms had a rather intimidating effect on them. Within moments order had been restored.

"Come on," said one of guards in a voice that indicated there would be no contradiction tolerated.

Nevertheless, Simon tried to intervene. "Sir, he's my brother, sir."

The guard stopped and looked in confusion at Worf and the Brikar. Since neither of them seemed a likely candidate, the guard asked, "Which one?"

"Him," Simon said, pointing to Worf. "And he was provoked. I saw the—"

"Doesn't matter," said the guard firmly. "We let the Commanding Officer sort this out."

"But—"

"Are you here to start as a cadet, son?"

"Yes, sir."

"In that case," said the guard, "I'm sure you have a passing familiarity with the concept of following an order. And I am ordering you now to move out of the way."

Simon looked at Worf helplessly, and Worf made a small gesture, waving Simon off. He mouthed, *It will be all right*. Not that he particularly believed it as the guards led him off to the C.O.'s office. The one consolation he took from all this was that the Brikar was in as much trouble as he was.

None of which was going to make it any easier, he thought, when he wound up being shipped home in record time. Who would have thought, when his parents brought him to the shuttle pad shortly after the wonderful farewell breakfast his mother had whipped up, that he'd be back home in time for dinner?

CHAPTER

3

Worf and the Brikar sat on opposite sides of the room. With their arms folded sullenly, and their legs outstretched, they looked like mirror images of each other. It was not a notion that Worf was particularly happy with—the thought that he might have anything in common with the obnoxious Brikar, including body language. So he shifted his position and crossed his legs.

Curiously, the Brikar had started to do the exact same thing. But, seeing that Worf was doing it, he promptly stopped and maintained his posture.

They sat that way, unmoving, for what seemed an eternity. They didn't speak to each other, and they even tried not to look at each other.

Finally, though, the silence weighed a bit too heavily on Worf's nerves . . . particularly when it was combined with the image he had in his head of his disappointed parents. "Why did you do it?" he demanded.

The Brikar looked up at him. "Do what?" he said blandly.

Worf made a noise of disgust. If the Brikar was going to play some sort of game with him, then Worf had no intention of participating.

But now, with the silence broken, the Brikar actually allowed himself a small smile of amusement. "Because I wanted you gone. Because you had no business being here. If it meant sacrificing my own place at the Academy, that didn't matter."

"I have as much business here as you," Worf shot back. "I had not done anything to you—"

"Like betray me," said the Brikar. "And now you won't have the opportunity."

At first Worf was going to pursue it, but then he saw the resolute, stubborn expression of the Brikar. The same look of hostility and intolerance he'd encountered so many times in the past. Here he had thought it was going to be different. What a tremendous disappointment to see how wrong he was.

The two of them said nothing further to each other, and then a door at the far end of the room slid open. A moment later a senior cadet stepped out. His face was unreadable.

More out of courtesy than out of a sense of duty—since both of the young individuals in the room had a suspicion that their Starfleet careers were over before they had begun—they rose and stood stiffly at attention.

"The admiral will see you now," was all the cadet said.

Worf and the Brikar moved past him and into the admiral's office.

The office itself was absolutely spotless. Nothing was

out of place. Trophies, awards, citations, mementos—all were neatly arranged. Small holos of the admiral standing next to a variety of top Starfleet officials lined shelves on the walls. All of them were regarding her with a look of affection.

The admiral sat behind a large desk, her fingers interlaced. The expression on her face left no doubt about how grave the situation was. Her face was round, her hair white. Her eyes were deepset, and her lips were drawn in a thin scowl of disapproval. For a moment Worf wondered if it was always that way, or whether she was just exceptionally irked for the occasion.

As the door hissed shut behind them, she let them stand there for a moment. She studied them, as if trying to decide at this very moment in time just how she was going to dispose of this case. Of course, Worf was quite certain that she knew precisely what she was going to do long before they'd entered.

He didn't understand what she was delaying for. How long could it possibly take to say, "You're both gone"?

She leaned back in her chair, her gaze never wavering. "Sit down, gentlemen," she said finally.

They sat, the tight leather of the Brikar's pants making an odd crinkling sound.

"I'm Admiral Fincher, Dean of Students," she said after a moment. "You gentlemen are . . . and I use the term loosely . . . cadets?"

The tone of her voice didn't seem to require, or even desire, an answer. So they gave none.

She shook her head and pushed aside a glowing computer screen. She fixed her gaze on the Brikar. "Zak Kebron," she said. "I did pronounce that correctly?"

"Yes, ma'am," he rumbled.

"You're only the third Brikar we've had at the Academy. Your test scores were exceptional. Your strength and reflexes were at the peak of the curve."

"Well," he said, casting a superior glance at Worf, "we Brikar *are,* after all, genetically bred for—"

"Be quiet," she said firmly.

Zak immediately became silent.

She turned her eyes toward Worf. "Worf Rozhenko," she said. "Our first Klingon." She leaned back, her fingertips pressed against one another. "I shipped out with your adopted father, back when we were both space rats just out of the Academy. He was quite a man."

"He still is," Worf replied.

She raised an amused eyebrow, giving the first, and only slightest, hint that she found any aspect of the situation at all amusing. "My apologies. I didn't mean to speak of him in the past tense." Then she paused and added, "Are you under the impression that my favorable history with your father is going to get you any special favors?"

"No, ma'am."

"Good. Well, gentlemen . . . one of the best pieces of advice I've ever heard is that you never get a second chance to make a good first impression. And the two of you have certainly blown that opportunity, eh?" Again she paused, and then she looked over at the computer screen. "It describes here," she said, "the psychological profiles of cadets Kebron and Rozhenko which lead inevitably to physical conflict. The Brikar have a historical dislike for Klingons, stemming from rather intense border battles that ensued between the races before the time of the great alliance. You must have heard some rather impressive horror stories about Klingons, eh, Kebron?"

He did nothing to hide his disgust when he looked at Worf. "Oh, yes."

"Um-hmm," said Fincher neutrally. "And you, Rozhenko, have run into individuals such as Kebron before. You have a history of altercations, making your little slugfest with Kebron here rather impossible to avoid."

"As always, I was provoked," Worf said. "I do not seek battle."

"But you won't walk away from it."

"That would not be honorable."

"Um-hmm," she said again. She drummed her fingers on her desk.

"With all due respect, Admiral," Worf said, "it is simple to look at the psychological profiles now and say that a fight was 'inevitable.' It would appear to relieve the Brikar of his responsibility in starting it, saying he had no choice due to upbringing—"

"Just as you had no choice in your response because of your origins, yes," said Fincher. "Look at the dates on this report, gentlemen."

She turned the computer around, and Worf and Zak leaned forward.

"Two months ago?" said Zak.

Fincher nodded slowly. "What appeared spontaneous to you gentlemen was something that we saw coming when we first accepted both your applications. The key to being a good Starfleet officer, Kebron . . . Rozhenko . . . is anticipating situations before they arise, and preparing for them. That's ninety-nine percent of what we teach

27

here—preparedness. If you go through life simply reacting to what happens, sooner or later the law of averages is going to catch up with you, and you will be overwhelmed by something you did not anticipate.''

She leaned back in her chair.

"Did you ever hear of 'The Cold Equations,' gentlemen?'' When they shook their heads, she continued. "It's a very famous short story, set during the early days of spacegoing. Back then every single pound that a ship was carrying had to be calculated perfectly, because the ship carried only enough fuel to get you where you needed to go. In that story a teenage girl stowed away aboard a small, one-person transport vessel because she wanted to see her brother on a colony world. Once the pilot discovered her, he realized her additional, unanticipated weight was going to eat up the fuel too fast. The result would have been a crashed ship, and a lost cargo . . . cargo that the colonists needed. The pilot had no choice but to jettison the girl. She died. The end. Now, it didn't happen. It's just fiction. However, it *could* very easily happen, given the right circumstances.

"The point, gentlemen, is that space is a very unforgiving environment. It's cold. It's airless. It is not charitable, and it does not make allowances for such things as bigotry and hostility. The vacuum of space doesn't care about your skin color, or your politics, or the strength in your arms, or the brains in your heads. You've got only two things going for you that can prevent a very swift, and very painful, death. The first is the integrity of your ship's hull. And the second is each other.''

She let that hang in the air for a moment.

"I admit to some degree of bias here,'' she said finally.

"I would be very, very disheartened to have to send the first Klingon ever to arrive at Starfleet Academy packing mere hours after he got here. That would be a bit of a failure, and failure is not something that I welcome. By the same token, I cannot allow Worf to stay and send you away, Kebron. That would not be fair."

"He started it!" Worf protested.

The admiral held up a stern finger. "I don't want to hear it," she said flatly. "This is not a schoolyard, gentlemen. This is not a playground. This is Starfleet Academy. Note the absence of playground equipment in the front courtyard. Note the large sign that says 'Starfleet Academy,' rather than a sign that reads 'This way to the monkey bars and seesaws.' That should have been your first clue."

She rose from her chair. Worf was struck by the fact that she was barely over five feet tall. It was rather surprising considering the amount of pure charisma she seemed to radiate: if she'd stood over six feet, that would have not surprised him.

She circled them slowly. "You've only got one thing in your favor. The fact that you have not yet checked in. Technically speaking, you aren't officially cadets until you sign in and register. You were still on your 'own time,' so to speak, when you chose to engage in that disgusting physical display in the courtyard. I can't sanction the actions of cadets who weren't cadets at the time of the infraction. Am I correct in assuming that you two would still like to attend this learning institution?"

They both nodded.

"Very well," she said. "However . . . as the records indicated, we did have an idea that this altercation might occur, although even we couldn't have anticipated the speed with which it would happen. Nevertheless, having expected it, we were able to make plans as to how to deal with it. Kebron . . . Rozhenko . . . look at each other.''

The Klingon and the Brikar slowly fixed each other with mutual glowers.

"Gentlemen," she said, "you're each looking at your new roommate.''

It took a moment for what she had said to sink in, and then they both spoke at once.

"Admiral, with all due respect—!''

"This is not going to work—!''

"I don't recall giving you gentlemen a choice," she said. "There are two questions, of course. The first is, how badly do you wish to remain at Starfleet? The second is . . . since I take it that you both find the situation intolerable . . . ?''

They nodded in unison.

"In that case, it's merely a question of which of you is going to resign first. As soon as one of you is gone, the other will have a much easier time of it, not to mention a room to himself. So . . . which of you is going to quit?''

The word hung there in the air, like a vulture. Neither of the young males quite knew how to react for a moment.

Then Worf said firmly, "I am not going to quit.''

"I have no intention of leaving," said Zak with equal certainty.

"Well, then!" said Fincher brightly. "It appears we'll all be one big, happy family then. One more such outburst as we endured earlier, however, and you will *both* be out.

I don't care about race, war stories, none of it. To put it in a way that I hope you'll understand: Now that you're in our playground, you'll play by our rules. Dismissed."

They turned and headed for the door.

"Oh, and gentlemen," she tossed after them. "Welcome to Starfleet Academy."

CHAPTER

4

By the time Worf had retrieved his bag from the shuttle pad and arrived at his quarters, Zak Kebron was already there.

Zak had unpacked his few belongings. A number of them seemed to be odd pieces of statuary and such, and they had been neatly arranged around the room.

Well, not "around," actually. They occupied precisely half the room . . . the right half. Stretched out on his bunk, a rock-like formation that must have been specially ordered for the Brikar, Zak did not even afford Worf a glance when the Klingon entered. Instead he spoke succinctly, in a manner that indicated he had already thought out precisely what he was going to say.

"Take careful notice," he said, "of the line."

And now Worf saw it: a long, black line that had been etched down the middle of the room, dividing it perfectly.

"This side," said Kebron, "is my side. The other side is your side. Keep everything of yours, including yourself, on that side, and everything should be fine."

"You are serious."

"Always," said Kebron.

For a moment Worf considered literally stepping over the line. But, he realized, that would be provoking a fight. He had always prided himself on not starting fights . . . only finishing them.

So he walked over to the other side of the room and tossed his suitcases on the bed. "I had hoped," he said, "to be rooming with my brother."

"I had hoped," replied Zak, "not to have to look at a Klingon face for the next several years. We don't all get what we ask for, do we."

"What is your problem?" Worf demanded in irritation.

"My problem?" Zak turned, propping himself up on one elbow. "My problem, Klingon, is that I know all about your kind."

"Oh, really?"

"Yes."

"And how many Klingons have you met, specifically?"

Zak frowned. "Just you," he admitted. But before Worf could comment on Zak's lack of familiarity with his people, Kebron quickly added, "But I've heard. I've heard plenty. My grandfather told me all about your kind. He told me about the wars. He told me that if you turn your back on a Klingon for a second, you'll find a knife in it. He told me about your evil rituals . . . about how you drink human blood, and your favorite meal is a human child."

Worf was appalled. "And you believed all that?"

"Are you calling my grandfather a liar?"

"Your grandfather was . . . misinformed," Worf said, not seeing any reason to pursue the matter further. "Tell me, Kebron, if you are so certain that Klingons are untrustworthy, why did you agree to room with me, then?''

"I wasn't exactly given a choice," Kebron pointed out. "And besides . . . I'm a very light sleeper. So don't try anything, Klingon, or we'll see just who winds up with a knife in him."

Worf went to his closet to put his things away. He discovered several Starfleet cadet uniforms already hanging there. They looked to be precisely his size. He shook his head in amazement. Anticipation, indeed! Not only had Admiral Fincher known precisely what she was going to do before she did it, but she had been quite certain of their agreeing to remain in a situation that neither of them thought particularly agreeable. So certain, in fact, that she had had their uniforms and a special bunk in their room, waiting for them.

He changed into his cadet uniform. This should have been a proud moment for him as he continued the Rozhenko tradition of Starfleet service. But it was marred by the look of disgust he got from Zak.

"I heard things about the Brikar, too, you know," said Worf. "Arrogant. High-handed. Blustering cowards, you were called. I have seen little from you to indicate any of that is an exaggeration. But as for you, you can look around as long as you wish, and you will never see me consuming a human baby."

With that, he walked out and down the hallway to try and find his brother.

He felt odd and self-conscious. It had taken him some time to come to terms with the fact that he would be the first Klingon in the halls of Starfleet Academy. But his less-than-stellar arrival had made him particularly sensitive. Every curious glance that he got, he interpreted as gaping. Every polite nod or brisk acknowledgment was (he quickly became convinced) merely a means of covering up some sort of hostility.

He knew that he couldn't go on thinking that way. He'd make himself crazy if he did. But he couldn't help himself.

"Worf!"

He turned to discover Simon, already in cadet uniform, running up behind him. His brother took him by the shoulders. "Here you are! I've been going crazy looking for you."

"I was not hiding."

"I know you weren't," said Simon with that easy laugh of his that Worf so envied. "I checked with the brass, and they told me that you hadn't been thrown out. I was so relieved! Not just for you, mind you," he said half-seriously. "I would have hated having to explain to Momma and Poppa how I didn't do a good enough job watching out for you. By the way, you missed our orientation speech and tour."

"I was unpacking."

"Your room assignment wasn't posted. Where are you rooming?"

"Section twenty-four, Room seven," said Worf. Then he added with obvious distaste, "They stuck me with the Brikar."

"No! The one you were fighting with?"

"Yes."

Simon shook his head. "Starfleet moves in mysterious ways. I'd thought we'd be roommates." He shrugged. "It's better than getting thrown out, I suppose . . .

although maybe not by much. Are you going to be okay?"

"I can stand it for as long as he can. Longer," he amended.

"Okay. Come on, I've got some people in my room I want you to meet."

"Are any of them Brikar?"

"No."

"Lead the way."

Simon led him to his own quarters. The first thing that Worf noticed when the door opened was that there was no line dividing it in half. Somehow that seemed a healthier way to go about things.

He also heard several voices all talking at once, but the noise abruptly ceased the moment Worf walked in. He recognized several of the occupants immediately.

"You're still here," Soleta the Vulcan said with interest. "How very intriguing."

"They acknowledged that I was not at fault," Worf said.

"More likely," replied Soleta, "they did not want to expel the first Klingon to attend the Academy. And they could not very well keep you and get rid of the Brikar. What did they do? Room you two together?"

Worf tried not to let the astonishment show on his face. "Yes."

"A logical course of action," she said.

"Mark over there is my roommate," said Simon, indicating the somewhat spaced Mark McHenry. "Mark's expertise is astronavigation. Isn't that right, Mark?"

Mark was busy making a hand puppet out of one of his socks.

Worf stared at him incredulously. "Astronav? Are you serious? He can barely find his way through the normal physical universe, much less chart a path through warp space. Put him at conn, and you will crash while still in dry dock."

"Come on, Worf, don't be so hard on the guy. Believe it or not, I hear he's a genius when it comes to—"

"Hi, everyone!" said Mark in a high-pitched voice, manipulating the mouth of his improvised puppet. "I'm Mark's sark! Or Mock's sock! Whichever!"

"When it comes to what?" said Worf dryly to Simon. "Ventriloquism? Bad news, Simon. I saw his mouth move."

"All right, all right. And this is Tania Tobias."

Simon stepped aside and an attractive young woman was just behind him. The first thing that Worf noticed about her was her eyes, which were large and shaped like a doe's. She had a small nose, and the general shape of her face could best be described as elfin as her jaw tapered down to a delicate point. Her skin was quite pale, almost alabaster, and her straight blond hair just touched her shoulders.

"It's a pleasure to meet you, Worf," she said. She shook his hand firmly.

"A pleasure to meet you, too."

"We were thinking of forming a study group. I was hoping you might want to join us," Simon told him.

"What a smashing idea!" said Mark's socked hand.

Worf cast him a cold glance. "Only if he leaves that in his closet."

Mark stared at the sock for a moment, and then asked, "Can I wear it on my foot?"

"Yes," said Worf impatiently.

Mark pulled the sock on over his boot—not out of any

attempt to get a laugh, but rather, Worf suspected, because he simply wasn't paying attention. Worf had the
sneaking suspicion that he wasn't going to have to worry
too much about McHenry being an irritating presence.
With his flakiness, it was likely that he'd be gone inside
of a week anyway.

"Tell you what," said Simon. "Let's go down to the
food lounge and get something to eat. Then we can go
over our various course schedules. Get things sorted out,
pinpoint our weak spots . . . that sort of thing."

Once again Worf felt a twinge of mild jealousy for his brother. Since arriving, Worf had managed to get into a wrestling match and be called on the carpet by the dean of students. In the exact same span of time Simon had organized a study group and was preparing to settle down to the business of getting things done. Worf was lucky to have him.

Worf headed for the door and walked out, taking the lead—

And the next thing he knew, something hard and metal had clattered down, enveloping his head, cutting off his vision, and, worst of all, sending water pouring down his uniform.

From behind him came gasps of shock, and from just in front of him was a roar of laughter.

Slowly he pulled the bucket off his head. An upperclassman was standing several feet away, doubled over with laughter, howling in joy. He was lean, with a shock of gray-white hair, and when he spoke it was with a thick Irish brogue.

"Beautiful!" he proclaimed, clapping his hands together in self-delight. "Oh, me great-grandfather, Sean Finnegan, would be so proud to know that his great-grandson is keeping alive the family tradition of practical joking! Oh, the jokes he played on young James Kirk will be nothing compared to me! Why, I—!"

Finnegan never saw what was coming. But the next thing he knew, he was regaining consciousness a day later in the infirmary. He had two less teeth, a black eye, and a broken nose, and he had to stay off solid foods for a week.

He wasn't able to swear out a complaint because he

was still dazed and wasn't sure what had happened. Nor did anyone else know . . . or, at least no one else was admitting that they knew.

He was relatively certain he'd been hit with something hard, like a brick of gold-plated latinum, for example.

Or a runaway shuttlecraft.

Either way, he never quite got up the nerve to pull a practical joke on anyone again. And he made particularly sure to give the whole study group a wide berth from then on.

CHAPTER

The course was Prime Directive—Theories and Application. It was one of the basic courses that all cadets had to master—filled with various case studies and scenarios that often led to lively, even bitter, debates among students. The Prime Directive was the first law of Starfleet. It stated that interference in the affairs and development of other planets and civilizations was forbidden. And it was the foundation upon which all other aspects of space exploration was based.

It was also Worf's first class.

When he entered the classroom, there was a general buzzing as the cadets talked with one another. He saw in their expressions everything from extreme nervousness to utter confidence.

The lecture hall angled downward, and stairways at either side led down to the lectern. Many of the seats farther back were already occupied as students followed the age-old custom of trying to sit as far back in the room as possible. There, they figured, the teacher would not be able to see them.

This strategy never worked, but it didn't stop students from trying it anyway.

As a result, Worf had to cover quite a bit of distance before he got to a row where there was an unoccupied seat. And he could not help but notice that, as he passed each row of students, the talking and buzzing ceased . . . to be replaced by hushed whispering.

Worf did not even glance at them, but he knew they were talking about him.

Then he did allow himself to look, and yes, indeed, they were stealing peeks at him. It was one of those situations where people desperately wanted to look, but they didn't want to be caught looking. As a result they made a tremendous show of trying to be subtle, but wound up being more obvious than ever.

Tania Tobias was seated about halfway down, and she waved to Worf. During the brief time he'd known her, Worf had been impressed by her genuine friendliness toward him. Naturally, being who he was, he was also suspicious. There were no empty seats in her row, though, so sitting next to her wasn't an option. He kept going.

He caught sight of Simon, who was seated midway across the third row from the front. Simon gestured for him to come over and sit beside him. For a moment Worf considered the option of distancing himself from his brother. Worf was clearly considered an oddity; why ruin Simon's reputation as well? But Simon was insistent, and the inevitable feeling of isolation got the better of Worf. He slid into place next to his brother.

"They are staring at me," Worf murmured in a low voice.

Simon shrugged. "Possibly. So what? You'll always be stared at, Worf. For now it's out of curiosity. Eventually it'll be out of admiration." He smiled that easy smile of his and punched Worf affectionately on the shoulder.

The far door opened, and the professor emerged. He bore a striking resemblance to an owl, from the beakish nose and tufts of white hair to the general slumped posture. This was Professor Lynch, and his reputation was legendary.

Lynch approached the lectern, turned, and regarded the class with a glare so piercing that it could have knocked down deflector shields.

There was no whispering now. Indeed, the only sound to be heard throughout the class was a series of nervous swallows.

Worf was impassive, however. Deep down, he was already convinced that he was not going to make it through the Academy. There were too many factors against him. It did not mean that he wasn't going to try his best. But, on the other hand, he wasn't going to be too surprised if it was ultimately decided that Starfleet wasn't ready for its first Klingon. And he would graciously accept failure when it came to him.

After all, the Klingon-Federation alliance had a long and tortured history since the Khitomer Conference of 2293. Every time a step forward had been taken, it seemed to be quickly followed by two steps back. It was barely a dozen years since the noble sacrifice of the *Enterprise NCC 1701-C*, which had been destroyed valiantly defending a Klingon outpost on Narendra III from a Romulan attack. That brave act had been the turning point of Klingon-Federation relations. But it was recent enough history that Klingons were still viewed askance by Terrans with short tempers and long memories.

Terrans . . . and Brikar. Worf glanced around, but he didn't see Zak anywhere. He must be taking the class at another time. For that Worf was grateful.

Professor Lynch had a padd in front of him that he consulted to check the students' names.

"In all my first-year classes, at this time," said Lynch, "I say the following words to my students. Listen carefully. These words will carry you through the difficult days and the long nights ahead. These words will serve you as you attempt to learn how to serve Starfleet. These words will give you strength as you watch, one by one, other classmates spiral down in flames. As you watch their hopes and dreams dashed by the demanding, rigorous, and sometimes overwhelming requirements of Starfleet Academy.

"And these words are: Good luck. You'll need it."

And then, without further preamble, he said, "Let us now examine the case of Eminiar VII. Mr. . . ." He glanced at his padd. "Mr. Rozhenko."

Worf and Simon both started to rise, and then looked at each other.

If Lynch was surprised, he didn't show it. "Ah. Twins, I assume."

A mild ripple of laughter drifted through the hall.

"Sir," Worf quickly said. "A request, if I may."

Lynch inclined his head slightly, indicating that Worf should continue.

"Among my people, the first name is used in all forms of direct address, including after honorifics such as *Mister*.

45

The house name, or surname, is reserved for formal occasions. To avoid confusion, I should be addressed as 'Mr. Worf.' ''

"Very well." Lynch tapped a notation into his padd, and immediately the request was updated on similar devices held by all the other teachers throughout the Academy. "Now, Mr. Worf . . . I was speaking to Mr. Rozhenko."

Again there was laughter. Clearly the students were in a good mood whenever there was amusement to be had at Worf's expense.

Worf sat, and Simon remained standing.

"Eminiar VII," said Lynch again.

Simon said nothing.

Puzzled, Worf looked up.

Simon's usual, ready smile was still there . . . but it was frozen on his face, with no sincerity behind it.

"Mr. Rozhenko!" said Lynch more loudly, even more forcefully. "We are waiting. Eminiar VII, if you please. This was assigned reading before you came to class. Did you read the case, Mr. Rozhenko?"

Simon's mouth moved, but no sound came out. And then he managed to find his voice. "Y-yes, sir. I read the text. I was . . . there were just so many case studies, I don't have that one at my fingertips. . . ."

Lynch came around from behind the lectern, his fingers resting lightly on it. "If you are in a life and death situation, *Mis-ter* Rozhenko, and you need Starfleet precedent to tell you what to do, do you think that you will be able to bring matters to a halt while you scan through your texts for the correct answer? Starfleet is not a court of law, *Mis-ter* Rozhenko. You will not be allowed the leisurely study of cases to prepare a brief. You must know things *instantly,* or it can cost you, or your crew, your life. Is that clear?''

Simon was sweating, his fingers wrapped so tightly around the edges of his desk that his knuckles were turning white. And Worf, as softly as he possibly could, whispered, "Kirk . . ."

"Kirk!" Simon fairly shouted. And then the words practically bubbled out of him. "The *Enterprise* went to Eminiar VII on a diplomatic mission. Eminiar was engaged in a computer-simulated war with their neighboring world, Vendikar. Computer-generated casualties were turned into real casualties through the voluntary suicide of the citizens upon being designated as fatalities."

Lynch nodded approvingly. "And what happened?"

"The *Enterprise* was registered as a casualty. Rather than submit his crew to be killed, Captain Kirk destroyed the computers of Eminiar VII, effectively ending the war."

"And he was wrong to do so, wasn't he?"

It stopped Simon cold. "Sir—?"

"Check the case, Mr. Rozhenko," said Lynch. "Eminiar tried to warn off the *Enterprise*. They issued a Code Seven Ten, forbidding contact. Kirk ignored it—an infraction of the Prime Directive right there. His violation resulted in the theoretical demise of his ship and crew. And then he destroyed Eminiar's entire way of life . . . an even more flagrant Prime Directive breach. Is that what you would have done?"

"Uh, no, sir," said Simon quickly, taking his cue from the scowling demeanor of his teacher.

His response prompted an incredulous gasp from

Lynch. *"What?* You would have ordered your crew to die, then? To voluntarily walk into disintegration chambers? What kind of cold-hearted commander would you have been? They might have mutinied! Did you consider that as you were shuffling them off to their deaths?"

"No . . . I mean, yes . . ."

Worf was stunned. He had never seen Simon this flustered . . . or flustered at all, as a matter of fact. And without thinking, he was on his feet. "Captain Kirk's actions were necessary, sir. Not right, nor wrong. Necessary."

"I was not speaking to you, Mr. Worf," said Lynch.

"No, sir. But I was speaking to you, sir."

There was a faint intake of breath from several of the cadets. Worf's response was perilously close to insubordination. But he had kept his voice as neutral—even respectful—as he possibly could.

Lynch's face darkened in a fierce scowl. And then he looked into the young Klingon's face and—in that brief moment—even saw a little into his heart.

And what he saw was a young male filled with respect for his teacher, and loyalty to his brother, and absolutely no fear for himself. It was an impressive combination.

The professor managed to keep some degree of that stern expression on his face. "Captain Kirk did have a choice."

"No, sir. He did not, because one of the two choices would have been tantamount to murdering his crew. No Starfleet officer—no man, if he is to call himself a man—would have made that dishonorable decision. That left him with one choice. And one choice, sir, is no choice."

Lynch was silent for a long moment. And then he said,

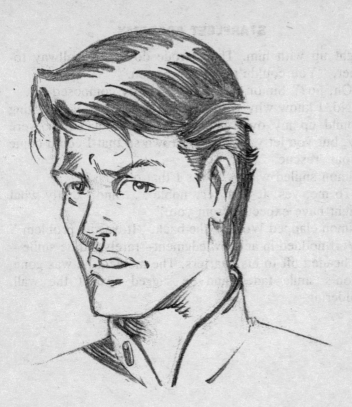

"Speak out of turn again, Mr. Worf, and it will be reflected in your grades. Take your seat—both of you."

They did so.

"Let us examine, moment by moment, the Eminiar VII scenario," said Lynch, "and see where potential disaster might have been averted. Mr. DelVecchio," he said, addressing Cadet Anita DelVecchio as "Mister" in accordance with Starfleet tradition, "we'll begin with you. . . ."

"I know why you did that," said Worf.

Simon had exited the classroom quickly, but Worf

caught up with him. They strode down the hallway together. "You couldn't fool me, Simon."

"Oh, no?" Simon now looked utterly composed.

"No. I know why you 'froze' in class. You were trying to build up my own confidence. Those questions were easy, but you let yourself be thrown so that I could come to your 'rescue.' "

Simon smiled wanly. "Was I that obvious?"

"To me, yes. It was very noble . . . and exactly what I might have expected from you."

Simon clapped Worf on the back. "It was no problem."

Worf nodded in acknowledgment—rarely did he smile—and headed off to his quarters. The moment he was gone, Simon's smile faded and he sagged against the wall, shuddering.

CHAPTER

None of the group had been quite able to believe it.

The legend of Mark McHenry had grown swiftly from the first time he'd opened his mouth in Basic Navigation class.

The instructor had thought she had found easy pickings in McHenry. The rest of the class had sat at rigid attention, trying with only limited success to grasp the fundamentals of astronavigation. Mark McHenry had looked as if he were somewhere else entirely. He sat there, staring at the overhead lighting as if it had sprouted wings.

The instructor was certain that McHenry was not paying the least bit of attention. She began to recite a long, complex problem that sent the entire class scrambling to their calculators. They tried desperately to keep up as she threw in variable after variable. Stray neutrinos, a quasar, a possible wormhole—all manner of deep-space phenomena that had to be accounted for when laying in the course. And as their fingers flew over the padds, McHenry just sat there with his chin in his hands, as if he were trying to watch passing electrons.

". . . and so," the instructor concluded, "you must reach your destination in precisely three days, nineteen hours, and forty-two minutes. What warp factor—to the thousandth place must—be maintained . . . *Mr. McHenry!*" she crowed triumphantly.

And without so much as a split-second pause, Mark replied, "Warp 4.735926."

The instructor's jaw dropped. Students using their data padds took at least another ten seconds to get the answer that Mark McHenry had just uttered off the top of his head.

As if noticing the teacher for the first time, Mark looked straight at her. "Oh . . . I'm sorry," he said, genuinely apologetic. "You did say thousandths. Just warp 4.736, then. I'm assuming you wanted that rounded off."

She nodded slowly, double-checking her own calculations with amazement. "Mr. McHenry . . . how in the world did you just do that?"

"Do what?" he asked in genuine confusion.

Rumor had it that the instructor had later pored over McHenry's files, convinced that he wasn't human. She was overheard muttering to another teacher, "I haven't felt that overmatched since that gold-faced android was a student here a dozen years ago."

Days had passed since that event. Mark continued to appear oblivious to the humor and unique aspect of his classroom performance. It had even taken his study group mates quite some time to fully grasp the way that the mind of Mark McHenry worked.

There were plenty of subjects at which Mark was only adequate at best. He had no head for deep philosophical

discussions, because he had trouble concentrating on them. Physically he was not particularly impressive, and the self-defense classes were nothing short of disastrous. He had a basic grasp of engineering, but that was about all.

But when it came to the realm of helm and navigation, it would have been an understatement to say that it was easy for him. In fact, it was too easy. Mark could plot courses and steer vessels with a speed that was matched only by computer . . . and computers didn't have human intuition to supplement them. Because it came easily to him, he simply did not devote a sizable portion of his brain or attention to it.

So he would daydream, or speculate, or work on coming to a fuller understanding of something that had previously eluded him. When instructors saw him in that state, they had first been under the impression that he was unaware of anything going on around him. They didn't realize that he was as aware as anyone else in the class, if not more so. It was quality of attention, not quantity, that was at issue. And when it came to quality, no one was able to approach Mark McHenry.

Now Mark was reclining in his favorite chair in his quarters, working with the rest of the study group as they labored over reviewing the week's lessons. If there was any frustration in dealing with Mark, it was that he had real difficulty explaining how he did what he did. He simply did it. Analyzing it was something that he was not very experienced with.

They'd been at it for three solid hours. Finally Simon leaned back and shut off his padd. "My head is swimming," he said, rubbing the bridge of his nose with his thumb and forefinger.

Mark looked up, interested. "Really? I would think they'd tend more to float, actually . . . since they don't have arms to swim. Or . . . well, in fact they'd probably sink rather than float, wouldn't they?"

Soleta, Worf, and Tania looked at him. Simon, who had long since gotten used to it, just leaned his head back.

Worf rose and said briskly, "I'll be going, then," and without another word walked out of the room.

"That was abrupt," said Tania.

"Typical," said Soleta, still looking over some text. "Klingons are an extremely moody species. Unfortunately, the moods range from bad to irritable."

"Be nice," Simon told her.

Soleta looked at him with eyebrow askance. "That is meant to be humorous, yes?"

Now Tania headed for the door. Soleta—who was her roommate—called after her, "Will you be out late tonight? I plan to meditate and will have the door sealed from 2100 to 2130 hours."

"You certainly have your life mapped out, don't you?" said Simon. "That's pretty amazing."

Soleta gave a small shrug. "To me, what is 'amazing' is that anyone would *not* have his or her life mapped out."

"Don't worry, Soleta," Tania said. "I won't disturb you. I have plans, too."

She walked out into the hallway and then, once the door closed behind her, murmured to herself, "Now, if only I knew what they were."

But she knew even as she said it. She knew before she started down the hallway that she was going to Worf's quarters. That she just wanted to talk to him.

She nodded politely to other classmates as she walked past them, but never strayed from the course that was going to lead her straight to Worf's quarters.

Soon she slowed, though, because she wasn't precisely sure which room was Worf's. But then she got a clue that tipped her off right away.

It was the sound of raised voices. One of them she immediately recognized as Worf's. The other she shortly identified as belonging to the Brikar cadet, Zak Kebron.

The voices were slightly muffled—but only slightly—

indicating that they were coming from inside a room. Tania noticed that the shouting match was drawing no reaction whatsoever from other passersby. She realized immediately that this was apparently so common in this particular area that cadets had gotten used to it.

"When are you going to get it through your oversize skull?" Zak demanded. "You are simply not welcome here!"

"I have every right to be here," Worf retorted.

"Rights! We're not talking rights! We're talking history. And historically, no one has ever trusted a Klingon! It is remarkable to me that you're vain enough to think you, singlehandedly, can change that!"

"No more vain than for you to think that you, single-handedly, can drive me from the Academy."

"Oh, I don't think that, Klingon. You've already made it painfully clear that, no matter what anyone says, you're going to continue to force your unwanted presence on us. Isn't that right?"

By this point Tania had found the room where the yelling was coming from. She stopped one passing student and asked, "Are they always like this?"

"Oh, no," replied the student. "Sometimes they're *really* loud."

Tania whistled. The student went on his way, and she stood outside the door, debating whether to ring the chime. But then she heard harsh footsteps coming toward the door. Feeling like a spy for some reason, she stepped back and flattened herself against the wall so that she wouldn't immediately be spotted.

The door hissed open, and Worf stormed out. His fists were clenched, his jaw set. His entire body was taut and quivering, and it was clear to Tania that he was doing everything he could to rein himself in. He never even spotted her as he turned to the right and stalked off down the hallway.

The sarcastic voice of Zak Kebron called after him, "Don't hurry back on my account!"

The door started to hiss shut, and Tania was faced with three choices: Follow Worf. Enter the room. Or go away and pretend that she hadn't been privy to any of the argument.

Acting purely on impulse, she stepped into Worf and Zak's quarters. The door halted in its slide shut, retreated briefly so that she could enter, and then closed.

From his desk, Zak Kebron glanced up at her and frowned, his heavy face developing small ridges in it. "Tobias, isn't it?" he asked.

She nodded.

He pointed to the door. "If you're looking for your Klingon friend, you just missed him."

She took a step forward. "Why do you hate him so much?" she demanded.

Zak leaned back, regarding her with interest. "Now, why in the world should you care about that? It's none of your concern."

"He's my friend. He's in my study group. If something affects him, then it affects me."

He made a low, somewhat amused-sounding cough. "Are you quite certain that's all it is?"

"What do you mean by that?"

"Oh, I've been watching you. How you always greet him so quickly. How you try to walk close to him without letting yourself be noticed. You like him."

"And you hate him."

"It's nothing personal. I hate all Klingons. What I can't comprehend is the sort of human that would become a Klingon friend."

Tania seemed to consider her response for a long moment. Then, slowly, she walked over to Zak and perched herself on the edge of his desk.

"You ever heard of Khitomer?" she asked him.

"Of course. The planet where they held the first major Klingon-Federation peace conference. The first in a long line of meetings with the Klingons that inevitably resulted in broken promises and threats of war."

"And you know nothing of it beyond that?"

"What's to know?"

"Well, I wasn't thinking of the Khitomer Peace Conference of 2293. I was thinking of the attack on Khitomer over half a century later."

"So there was an attack," said Zak. "So what?"

She regarded him for a moment, as if debating whether to tell him or not. Clearly, though, having come this far, she could not go back. "There was a Klingon outpost there, and Romulans attacked it. No one is sure why. The general speculation was that, in Romulan time-keeping, it represented some sort of anniversary of the peace conference. The Romulans and Klingons were allies once—"

"Never did any two races so royally deserve each other," said Zak.

"—and the breakup of that alliance was a very sore point between them. It caused many years of fighting. Anyway, the Romulans decided to make Khitomer a target, and they massacred the inhabitants. It was a sneak attack. Four thousand Klingons, Zak . . . *four thousand* . . . died in the slaughter. Men. Women. Children. Romulan plasma weapons didn't distinguish by age or gender."

"As if the Klingons cared about *their* victims," said Zak. But he didn't say it with his usual bluster. As much as he disliked Klingons, the thought of such butchery was extremely distasteful.

"My father," she continued, "was serving on board the starship *Intrepid* when they received a distress call. They got to the planet, but too late. The damage was done. Bloodied bodies everywhere . . . as far as the eye could see. It had been a science outpost, Kebron. It was doing no harm to anyone. But that made no difference to the Romulans. They killed everyone they could anyway."

She paused to let the image sink in. "The *Intrepid* beamed down hundreds of crew members to help in the cleanup and to try and save lives wherever they could. My father had been on very few away teams . . . he was an engineer. But the captain pressed all able-bodied crew members to help out. He told me . . . so many times, he told me . . . that he had never seen anything like it. And the thing that struck him the most was how brave the Klingons were. No moaning. No sobbing. No one begging, 'Help me, please!' To all intents and purposes they had been massacred, but nevertheless the survivors were unbowed.

"He told me about one Klingon woman. As soon as they pulled her out from under the rubble, she immediately pitched in digging out others. He didn't find out until later that she had a broken arm and two broken ribs. She just kept right on going, ignoring the pain."

"Is there some point to all this?" said Zak, trying his best to sound impatient.

As if he hadn't spoken, Tania continued. "And there
was one incident in particular that I remember. My father
was passing by a pile of rubble along with a fellow crew
member—a warp-field specialist named Sergey Rozhenko.
And there was a little hand sticking out from under the
debris. They figured that whoever the hand belonged to
was dead. But then Rozhenko saw the hand move, just a
little bit. As if it were struggling with whatever small
strength it had left to push the rubble off.

"Rozhenko ran over to the pile and shoved it off. My

father helped him. And there . . . burned, battered, and newly made into an orphan . . . was a six-year-old Klingon boy.

"He didn't utter a sound. There wasn't so much as a tear on his face. When Rozhenko asked where his parents were, he was able to lead them right to them. Well . . . to the half ton of rubble he thought their bodies were under, at any rate. Finally Rozhenko said to him, 'What's your name?' And the little Klingon boy said, 'Worf.'

"Now, Zak Kebron . . . compare your early life to that of young Worf Rozhenko. You talk of how your race has suffered. But what about you personally? And how does your suffering stack up next to what Worf went through?"

Zak Kebron said nothing.

Tania slid off the desk and headed for the door. She stopped there, paused, and turned to face him. "Now, I'm not going to tell you what to do, Zak. But if I were you, I might consider easing up on Worf . . . just a bit. Because, let's face it. If you think you're going to be able to hurt him, then you're kidding yourself. Compared to what he's lived through, anything that you could possibly throw at him would be minor league."

Then she walked out, leaving Zak Kebron alone with his study materials.

CHAPTER

7

A few weeks later Worf walked across the cafeteria, carrying the tray with his lunch on it.

A special replicator program had been created to simulate Klingon foods. The flavor wasn't exactly right, though, and Worf was not especially thrilled with the results.

It was a sentiment shared by his fellow cadets. They had long gotten past their initial revulsion whenever Worf happened to get near with his lunch. But he wasn't exactly a welcome lunch companion. Rarely did anyone ever stand up and wave and shout, "Worf! Bring your plate of nauseating wormlike crawling things over here!"

For a while there Cadet Stanislaw was trying to lose weight. So he made a point of eating every meal as near to Worf as he could. Looking at Worf's food always killed Stanislaw's appetite, and in no time at all he had dropped fifteen pounds. Once he'd reached his goal weight, however, he went back to eating near cadets with less repulsive lunches.

So Worf usually wound up eating with Simon, who was at least accustomed to the Klingon's eating habits.

He put his tray down opposite his brother's. "How are you?" he asked, without really looking at Simon. But when he did, he blinked in surprise.

Simon was asleep.

Clearly he had merely intended to rest his eyes for a moment. He sat with his head propped up on his fist. But now, there he was, softly snoring.

"Simon!" whispered Worf harshly, and he prodded his brother. Simon jumped slightly, his eyes snapping open, and he looked around a moment in confusion.

"Huh—?"

"Simon, what is the matter with you?"

"Oh." He rubbed his eyes with his fists, trying his best to shake the sleep out of them. "Just put in a late night, that's all."

Worf looked at him askance. "Late night? The study group broke up at 2300 hours. How much later did you stay up past then?"

"Another three . . . four hours . . ."

"Why?"

"There were some things I didn't get, okay? Some warp sine ratios that were a bit hard to follow, that's all."

Worf was dumbfounded. "I thought we all were clear on that. You did not give any indication that—"

"I didn't want to slow everyone down, okay? I have it now. I'm clear on it. There's nothing more that has to be said about it, all right?"

It was all very strange to Worf. The warp sine ratios were basic stuff. Worf was no genius when it came to such things, but even he had gotten a handle on it fairly quickly.

And then he realized that it was just Simon being Simon. Simple understanding was never good enough for him. Surely Simon had grasped the fundamentals immediately. Knowing him, what he was busy doing now was working ahead, trying to stay one jump in front of the students and possibly even the teacher. Yes, that would be typical behavior for him. While the others were getting the basics straight, Simon was light-years ahead learning the advanced stuff.

In fact . . . he was probably doing it so that, when Worf hit a snag (as would inevitably happen), Simon would already be thoroughly versed in the material so that he could help Worf along.

Because that was the sort of considerate brother that Simon was.

"All right, Simon," said Worf gamely, not wanting to indicate to Simon that he'd figured out what he was up to. "All right."

Mark McHenry dropped into place next to them, his tray rattling loudly as he sat down. He looked at Simon and Worf intently. "Why *isn't* there a word that rhymes with *orange?*" he asked.

The Rozhenko brothers stared at each other.

And then an upperclassman called out loudly, "*Cadets!*"

It was a tone of voice that they recognized immediately. They leapt to their feet, snapping to full attention.

Superintendent Sulak entered and strode to the front of the cafeteria. The cadets remained on their feet, looking neither left nor right. Sulak reached the front and turned to face them.

"As you were," said the imposing, deep-voiced Vulcan. The cadets immediately took their seats, then remained motionless, waiting patiently for Sulak to speak.

"Professor Lupisky," he said, "has been in an air vehicle accident. Fortunately it was not fatal, but the professor will be out of commission for the rest of the week."

"We have his Combat Strategy class next period," Worf said in a low voice to Simon.

"I guess you don't," McHenry replied, equally softly.

"Quiet, please," said Sulak, prompting Worf to wince in chagrin at having forgotten the sharpness of Vulcan ears. "Now, then . . . far be it from Professor Lupisky to give all of you a week off. Therefore, in place of his class time—and, in fact, during your spare time—each of you is to prepare a paper on the following topic. Two years ago, Captain Jean-Luc Picard, while in command of the USS *Stargazer,* was ambushed in the Maxia Zeta star system. He improvised a combat technique which has been nicknamed the Picard Maneuver. This unprecedented procedure resulted in the survival of his crew, although it did result in the loss of the vessel itself. Your assignment is to select twenty significant battles in Starfleet history. Then suggest how they might have ended differently had the Picard Maneuver been in existence at the time. That is all."

Without another word, Sulak turned and walked out of the cafeteria. The moment Sulak was gone, the cadets started murmuring to each other, discussing which battles they might write about.

"Mind if I join you?"

Simon and Worf looked up and saw Tania standing there holding a tray. Simon slid aside as Tania seated herself.

"I heard my father talking about that whole *Stargazer* business," said Simon. "Picard was court-martialed, I heard."

"I am not surprised," said Worf. "A captain should go down with his ship. I could never serve under such a man."

"Worf, did it ever occur to you that you might not be given a choice of who you serve under?" said Tania with a smile. "Besides, as I recall, the court-martial didn't result in a conviction. So obviously Starfleet felt that his actions were not out of line."

"Well," said Worf stiffly. "There are many variables that go into a court-martial. Who knows what sort of tactics the defense lawyer used."

"Oh, yes," said Tania. "Maybe the lawyer did something underhanded like . . . oh . . . having testimony from the crew members who owed their life to Picard's ingenuity."

Worf made a dismissive noise. "It is pointless to discuss it," he said. "The entire matter is moot."

She shrugged. "Okay. Do you want to work on our projects together?"

She was looking at him with those large doe eyes of hers. Worf merely replied, "Perhaps. We can discuss it later. If you will excuse me . . ."

He rose and started out the room. Simon turned to Tania and said, "Be right back," and then headed after his brother.

"Worf!" he said in a whisper, drawing alongside him. "Does someone have to hit you over the head with a rock or something?"

Worf looked at him in confusion. "I hope not. Why?"

"Tania, Worf! The way she looks at you! The way her voice gets softer whenever she talks to you!"

Worf frowned. "I do not understand—"

"She's crazy about you, Worf! You spend so much time scowling that you're totally missing what's happening in the world around you!"

"Nonsense," said Worf firmly. "She has no particular feeling for me."

"Yes, she does!"

"And even if she did . . . she is human. I am Klingon."

"You're a Klingon, raised by humans! If she's interested in you, you should pursue it!"

He took Simon firmly by the shoulders. "Simon . . . at most, I would be an object of curiosity for her. That is all. I will not be a—what is the phrase?—a guinea pig for her to experiment on. If she is feeling inquisitive, let her inquire elsewhere."

Before Simon could say another word, Worf turned and walked out of the cafeteria.

CHAPTER

Commander Clark was one of the foremost experts in hand-to-hand combat in all of Starfleet. He walked with a confidence and swagger that Worf could not help but admire.

The cadets were dressed in loose-fitting workout uniforms. They were seated in a circle on the floor, their legs crisscrossed in the lotus position.

Clark walked around the circle, his hands draped loosely behind his back. He was broad-shouldered, muscular. His hair was gray and cropped to reveal a widow's peak. His hands looked like slabs of meat, and the muscles on his legs appeared finely carved, like marble. Worf watched him carefully, making mental notes of his every move. Seated across from Worf in the circle was Zak Kebron. Worf tried not to look at him. Bad enough that he had to stare at him all the time in their shared quarters.

"Thus far," Clark was saying, "we have been training in unarmed combat. You cannot allow yourselves to become dependent simply on phasers—particularly those of you who are intending to specialize in security duty. You must be able to disarm and handle opponents without automatically resorting to shooting them. Are we all clear on that?''

There were nods from around the circle.

''We've been focusing on the basics of tae kwon do for offense, since its reliance on the use of legs gives you an extended reach. And we've been using aikido to build a defense system, since aikido is tremendously effective in turning your opponent's strength aside. There are many types of life-forms out in the galaxy . . . many of them with strength far higher than Terran norm.''

Zak nodded in approval at the words. Worf said nothing but merely ''harrummphed'' mentally.

''There are also,'' said Clark, ''many weapons, which you must be versed in. You never know when you're going to be drawn into a personal combat situation. And there may even be times when such combat is ritualistic and obligatory in the society you're visiting at the time. The Prime Directive instructs us to obey local customs whenever possible. Duels and such are not something you'll run into every day but, they are possibilities that you must be prepared for.

''This aspect of the self-defense course was one introduced by Admiral James T. Kirk himself during his tenure teaching at the Academy. In his voyages he had to handle a variety of weapons. Fortunately, the admiral was a very quick study, and that saved his life. But he—and we—believe in being prepared.''

Clark walked over to a supply closet and pulled out two

long staffs. Simple wooden staffs, but nevertheless they looked potentially vicious.

"A number of weapons throughout the galaxy are variations on the ancient Terran weapon called the quarterstaff. The Vulcans, for example, have the *lirpa*, which has the rather intriguing additions of a bludgeon at one end and a fairly vicious blade on the other. The Pamanians have the *syzke*, which has shredded sheets of cloth at either end. That may sound absurd until you realize that they're very effective for momentarily blocking your vision. And in personal combat, losing sight of your foe for even a moment can result in a very quick end to the combat . . . and, if you're unlucky, to you." Out of the corner of his eye, he noticed Worf looking as if he had something to say. "Yes, Mr. Worf?"

Worf was thinking of the *bat'telh*, the bladed Klingon weapon that was also very similar to the quarterstaff. It was, in fact, a weapon that he was rather experienced with. It was one of the few possessions that had been salvaged from Khitomer. It had belonged to his father—his Klingon father, Mogh—and Worf had practiced with it zealously every day of his life.

At first Helena Rozhenko had been terrified of the weapon—particularly the vicious hissing noise it made as the blade cut through the air. She began "accidentally" misplacing it, but Worf would always find it within a day or so. Finally, in exasperation, she had said, "Fine! But if you cut off a leg, don't come running to me!" Young Worf hadn't even bothered to point out the contradiction in that. He was too busy practicing.

Nevertheless, he abruptly felt self-conscious. If he described his own experience, he would draw attention to the notion that he himself was a member of one of those "alien" races with bizarre weapons that they were preparing for.

"Just . . . shifting position, sir," said Worf slowly.

"I see." Clark turned his attention back to the class. "If you understand the basics of how to use the quarterstaff, it will serve you well should you find yourself in a situation where you have to use similar weapons."

He held a quarterstaff out in front of him, horizontally. "You place your hands here and here," he said, indicating places near the midpoint of the staff. "Don't grip it tightly. Now . . . to bring up one of the ends, you keep one hand stationary and slide the other hand inward, like so . . ."

In about fifteen minutes Clark had outlined the fundamental quarterstaff moves. Then he surveyed the ring of students. "Mr. Worf, you'll be my first victim. I hope you've shifted position enough to keep you limber."

Worf rose and took a place within the circle. The other cadets backed up slightly to provide more room. He picked up the other quarterstaff and, balancing it confidently in his hands, poised on the balls of his bare feet and faced Clark.

Clark came in fast, feinting. Worf made a small motion as if he believed that the feint was, in fact, the real move. So when Clark brought the end of his staff around with his genuine attack, Worf had not committed himself and was able to sidestep with ease.

Clark, who had been overconfident, missed clean. He was momentarily off-balance, and Worf brought the staff up fast and slammed it against the pit of Clark's stomach.

Clark made a *whufff* noise and went down to his knees, gasping.

The entire exchange had taken no more than five seconds. It took almost that long again for the students to register what had happened. Automatically the other cadets started forward to help him, but Clark managed to wave them off.

"Worf, help him up!" said Cadet Briggs.

Worf stared at him in mild surprise. Helping Clark up had never occurred to him. If a warrior was felled, it was considered dishonorable to extend a hand to him. The implication would be that the fallen warrior was weak and unable to fend for himself. The honorable thing to do—as long as it wasn't a life and death situation—was to stand perfectly still. To wait for the downed opponent to compose himself and state whether he wished to continue.

"Why?" asked Worf.

"Because it's the right thing to do!" said another cadet angrily. "What, Klingons don't help each other up?"

"No," he said matter-of-factly.

He looked around slowly and, instead of admiration, saw the look of barely restrained contempt in their faces.

They hated him. They all hated him.

Clark, who had managed to recover his voice, finally said, "It's okay. I'm fine. Mr. Worf," he said grudgingly, "it seems I've allowed myself to get sloppy—and you didn't let me get away with it. Good for you." He slowly straightened up.

"Thank you, sir."

Then Clark noticed that Zak Kebron was scowling fiercely . . . more fiercely than ever before, which was something of an accomplishment. "Mr. Kebron, you think you can do better against Mr. Worf?"

"Yes," was all he said.

Clark waved for him to get up, and Zak did so. The instructor handed him the quarterstaff, and then Clark sat down off to the side, nursing his bruised stomach.

Zak Kebron held the staff with confidence and faced Worf. "This time," he said, "you're going to get hurt."

"If you are able," Worf replied indifferently.

Clark looked up, suddenly remembering. He hadn't been present that first day of the school year when Worf and Zak had gotten into a fistfight. There was genuine bad blood between the two of them, but he'd only heard about it secondhand. And that was a few weeks ago, so it wasn't fresh in Clark's mind—especially when he'd just gotten his teeth rattled by the Klingon's staff.

Having the Klingon and the Brikar battle now, with weapons, was an extraordinarily bad move. Clark immediately started to shout for them to stop.

It was too late.

The weapons slammed together. The cadets immediately began shouting encouragement, in voices so loud and raucous that the still breathless Clark couldn't make himself heard.

The first exchange of blows was so rapid that no one except the two combatants could follow it. The air was alive with the rapid *clack clack* of the wood on wood.

For the first moments of the encounter, Worf calmly sized up the tactics of his opponent. Zak seemed to be depending on his size and strength to carry the day.

Zak pressed the attack, and Worf allowed himself to be driven back. Then Worf ducked under one particularly fierce blow and brought his staff up quickly, slamming Zak in the stomach.

The Brikar staggered only slightly and recovered much

faster than Worf had anticipated. He charged forward, and Worf was barely able to block the thrust.

They stood there a moment, shoving and grunting, pushing against each other, neither giving ground. The cadets were cheering and shouting—but no one was calling out Worf's name. If the lack of support bothered him, he didn't let it show.

Worf twisted and Zak's staff slid off, momentarily unbalancing him. Worf chose that moment to try and end it—he reversed his quarterstaff and slammed it down.

But Zak deflected Worf's quarterstaff and, in that moment, switched tactics and drove a furious kick to Worf's stomach.

Worf had a split second to react to it, and he managed to twist himself around and catch some of the impact with his sturdy rib cage. He spun with the force of the blow and dropped to one knee. As Zak's quarterstaff whistled above his head, cutting an arc in the air, Worf jammed his quarterstaff in between Zak's legs. Before Zak realized what was happening, Worf pulled back on the quarterstaff, using it as a lever. It sent Zak's feet right out from under him, and he thudded to the floor with such a powerful crash that it seemed to shake the gymnasium.

Like a bolt of lightning, Worf was straddling him, his quarterstaff across Zak's throat and pushing down. "Surrender," grated Worf.

Zak said nothing. He glowered fiercely at Worf and tried to push him off. But he couldn't get the leverage to do it.

"That's enough, Mr. Worf," Clark now said. "Get off him now."

Slowly Worf stepped back. Zak got to his feet, refusing

to show any sign of weakness such as rubbing any bruised parts of his body.

"Shake hands," said Clark.

They looked at him.

"Now," Clark said with no undue emphasis, and added, "That was not a request, gentlemen."

The two of them shook hands. But Worf could see from the way that Zak was looking at him that he was filled with anger and hostility. And he could also see, from the way that the other students were staring at him, that he didn't have a lot of hope for winning a popularity contest in the near future.

"Put the quarterstaffs back, gentlemen," said Clark. He clapped his hands briskly, and Worf and Zak replaced the staffs in the closet.

For the rest of the period, Zak said nothing to Worf. Nor did anyone else.

CHAPTER

When Professor Lupisky, looking none the worse for wear and no less crotchety, strode to the front of his class a week later, the cadets burst into applause. He waved it off, trying to look as if the display of respect was irritating him. In fact, he was extremely flattered by it, but he would hardly be inclined to let on.

"So," he said in that clipped German accent for which he was so renowned, "you have been working hard, yes? During my enforced vacation? Superintendent Sulak conveyed to you my instructions for independent research?"

Heads bobbed all over the room.

"Good. So there will be no one saying things like, 'I had not heard about it' or 'I didn't know' or any other such utter wastes of breath and time."

Heads shook all over the room.

"Very well. Famous battles, then, that would have come out differently had the Picard Maneuver been put into play. Who would like to go first?"

Worf raised his hand immediately, double-checking his padd notations to make certain that he had his information down correctly. He glanced over at Simon. Simon didn't have his hand raised. Typical. Not wanting to jump to the forefront.

"Mister . . ." Lupisky checked his charts. "Kebron."

Zak Kebron, several rows back and to the right, rose.

"The first battle I chose," he said, "was the Rimbor Engagement in the year 2264. The USS *Farragut* was confronted by three Klingon vessels."

Slowly Worf turned in his seat to fix Zak with as vicious a stare as he could muster.

If Zak noticed, he didn't indicate it. "The *Farragut* sustained heavy casualties . . . seventy-nine dead, eighty-three more injured. They managed to disable one of the three Klingon warships and barely escape. If, however, the captain had employed the Picard Maneuver at exactly forty-two seconds into the engagement, my calculations show that he could have completely destroyed two of the three Klingon war vessels. The third Klingon vessel would doubtless have run at that point because . . . well . . . that's how they are."

"That's how who are, Mr. Kebron?" asked Lupisky. There was a dangerous tone in his voice.

"Klingons, sir. They generally run unless they outnumber their opponents two to one."

"*That is a lie!*" Worf fairly roared.

"Mr. Worf, control yourself," Lupisky snapped, but he didn't seem any too pleased with Zak, either. "Mr. Kebron, such overwhelming racial slurs will not be tolerated—"

"With all due respect, sir," Zak said mildly, "it's not

intended as such. Out of the one hundred and seventy-three different engagements with Klingons that I studied for this report—"

"You *only* studied Klingon skirmishes?" said Lupisky incredulously. "You mean with all the hostile races that have been encountered—Rigelians, Cardassians, Ferengi, Orions, Romulans, Tholians, Gorn—with *all* of them and many more, you only saw fit to study battles involving Klingons?"

"I like to specialize, sir," was the calm response.

"Sit down, Mr. Kebron." Lupisky's voice dropped the temperature in the room by at least twenty degrees. "Someone else, please. Mr. Briggs."

Cadet Briggs now rose, and Worf suspected what was coming.

He was right.

"The Battle of Chernobog," began Briggs, "involved the ambush of a freighter convoy by—"

"Klingons," Lupisky cut him off. "Do you have *any* scenarios that did not involve a Klingon battle?"

Briggs consulted his padd and pretended to look surprised. "Why . . . no, sir."

Lupisky slowly surveyed the class. There was cold fury in his eyes. "May I ask how many people here worked up studies of battles that did *not*—repeat, *not*—involve Klingons?"

Worf raised his hand, as did Simon. Tania, the only other member of their study group in the class, was in the front row. She raised her hand.

Everyone else sat in stony silence.

Worf rose, gathered up his padd, and headed for the exit.

"Mr. Worf, I did not give you permission to leave," Lupisky called after him.

Worf stopped at the door, turned, and said, "With all due respect, Professor . . . I did not ask your permission." And then he walked out.

There was a long silence. Cadets glanced at each other, smirking slightly.

Lupisky wasn't smirking.

He was furious.

"That," said Lupisky, "was the most abominable display I have ever seen by any Starfleet class. Ever. In my entire career"—and his voice rose, driven by his bubbling anger—"in my entire career I have never witnessed intentional collusion for the single and sole purpose of humiliating a fellow classmate. Your behavior was scandalous. Scandalous! Correct me if I am wrong, but you people have entered this Academy because you want to uphold our oath. To seek out new life and new civilizations. Well, ladies and gentlemen, the fellow whom you just humiliated into leaving this room is—as far as you are concerned—a new life. The vast majority of you have never even *met* a Klingon. Yet you had the nerve to come in here with your prejudices and your predispositions and drive him away! What you just did was shocking and completely inappropriate for anyone who has any desire to serve in Starfleet!"

"Sir," Zak spoke up, "if I may, you didn't tell us that we *couldn't* focus on—"

"Quiet, Mr. Kebron!" snapped Lupisky. "Don't insult my intelligence. We both know that this was no coincidence. This was a concerted effort, and I find it repulsive. Repulsive! And with the exceptions of Mr. Rozhenko and Mr. Tobias, I certainly hope that you people have no aversion to *plenty* of extra work. Because I can guarantee you that that is what you have just bought yourselves."

A low moan echoed through the class, and a number of angry stares were directed at Zak. That was more than enough to tell Lupisky just precisely who had been the organizer of the little stunt.

But Zak didn't care. Because he was hoping that maybe finally—*finally*—Worf was getting the message. With any luck, by tomorrow the Klingon would be long gone.

For just a brief moment he felt a flash of guilt, recalling the things that Tania had said. But then he thought of what had happened in the self-defense class, and he remained convinced that he had done exactly the right thing.

Worf Rozhenko was, quite simply, not the kind of cadet that Starfleet wanted or needed.

Worf barreled down the corridor, pushing past any cadets who happened to get in his way. When they caught a look at Worf's angry expression, their immediate responses to the less-than-gentle treatment were quickly stifled.

He burst out of the building, moving so quickly that the doors barely had time to open for him. In the mood that he was in, it was very likely that if the doors had not been open, he simply would have gone straight through them.

He stood outside the Academy and finally allowed himself to lean back against one of the great walls. He fought to slow the racing of his heart and the pounding of his pulse against his temple.

He was not sure which he was more angry about: The fact that they had organized this charming little reminder of the hostile history of Klingon-Federation relationships. Or the fact that he had let them rattle him so.

Rattle him? Who was he kidding?

There was no point to this. None at all.

If he had any brains in his head, he would head back to his quarters, pack his things, and be out the door for good before anyone came back from class.

Of course he was a fighter. Of course he was tough.

But through much of his life, whenever he had encountered suspicion and hostility, there had been a hope that somehow, somewhere, it might get better.

Starfleet had crystallized that hope for him.

And now it was all falling apart.

What in the world was the reason for shoving himself into a situation where he was very clearly not wanted?

He heard a soft footfall nearby him, and his head snapped around. He frowned in puzzlement at the intruder.

It was a young man, several years older than Worf, standing near the bushes. Worf could see that he was wearing some sort of odd eye gear . . . sunglasses, perhaps. Maybe his eyes were particularly sensitive to the light.

He was staring fixedly at Worf, standing several feet away.

"What is the matter?" demanded Worf.

The young man's head tilted slightly, as if he were turning his head in the direction of Worf's voice. "I'm sorry. Are . . . I hope this doesn't sound rude. You're not human, are you?"

Worf opened his mouth in amazement, and then closed it. "Are you joking?"

"I don't think so."

"I am a Klingon!" he said incredulously. "What are you, blind?"

The other man smiled lopsidedly. "Well, uh, yes, as a matter of fact. From birth."

He came around the bush, and now Worf saw, to his chagrin, that the young man was wearing an ensign uniform.

He stuck out a hand. "I'm Geordi La Forge."

"Worf," he replied, shaking the hand firmly. He stared at La Forge's face. "That . . . device on your face. It enables you to see?"

"After a fashion," said Geordi. "I'm still getting used to it. It's called a VISOR. I see things . . . a little differently than most people. That's why I was staring at you. I was picking up thermal readings from you that weren't even close to the norm."

"No," said Worf, sounding dangerously close to self-pitying. "Nothing about me is the 'norm.' That is something that I am very frequently reminded of."

Geordi tilted his head again, and Worf quickly realized that it was a reflex La Forge had developed through years of sightlessness. "Sounds as if you're having some sort of problem, Worf. You're attending the Academy, right?"

"First year," Worf acknowledged.

Geordi nodded. "I just graduated. I'm waiting for my first posting. So, what's the problem? Work load getting you down? Maybe a study group—"

"I am coping with the work load quite adequately, thank you. Your concern is appreciated. I will take up no more of your time."

"Now, wait a minute—"

"Thank you, Mr. La Forge."

Worf started to walk away from the building, but Geordi called from behind him, in a sharp and firm voice, "Cadet, halt!"

Reflexively, even though he would have preferred to keep going, Worf stopped in his tracks.

Geordi came up behind him, walking casually. "Now, you want to tell me what the problem is?"

"With all due respect, sir . . . no. I can deal with the situation on my own."

"Really? How are you planning to do that? By quitting?"

Worf looked at him in surprise. "Who told you that?"

Geordi started down one of the paths. "Let me guess. You're feeling alienated. Separate from your classmates."

"They are making it . . . difficult," Worf acknowledged, falling into step beside him.

"Yeah, well, there's no excuse for that," said Geordi readily. "The only thing I can say to that is that the reason people come to the Academy is to learn. And what you're learning here is a lot more than facts and figures, ship names and stardates. You're all learning a particular way of thinking. Look . . . Worf, was it?"

Worf nodded, and then realized he wasn't certain if the VISOR was subtle enough to detect such small gestures. So he said "Yes," almost as an afterthought.

"Worf, there's a lot of stuff that people think automatically. A lot of presumptions, a lot of built-in mechanisms. At Starfleet Academy, people are asked to unlearn many things that have been ground into us, almost from the time that our ancestors—or my ancestors, at least—were squatting around the first fires, looking nervously at the glowing eyes in the forest. And one of the most fundamen-

tal of those built-in mechanisms is that people are afraid of things that they don't understand. They're afraid because they think that the unknown could hurt them.

"The whole key to being a good Starfleet officer," continued La Forge, "is not to be afraid of the unknown, but instead to embrace it. To be drawn to it, to study it. To be excited by it and want to share in its wonders. Believe it or not, that's not an easy transition to make. And in the midst of your classmates trying to make that transition to embracing the unknown, here you are. The unknown, in the flesh. Worse than the unknown—they figure they know everything they need to know about Klingons, and they're nervous about what they do know."

"You are not nervous," said Worf.

Geordi shrugged. "Why should I be? We're at peace with the Klingon Empire. You're here at the Academy, and I presume they wouldn't let you in unless they'd checked you out. So I doubt you're a crazed killer or anything. Are you?"

Worf actually smiled, ever so slightly, at the engaging tone in La Forge's voice. "Not to my knowledge."

"Well, then . . . ?"

"But I am different from them," said Worf. "I think differently, act differently. And they—"

"Are students," Geordi reminded him. "Still learning. Still growing. Just as you are, believe it or not. And just as they're going to come to learn about the special requirements of Klingons, you are going to come to the understanding that humans sometimes need special handling as well. Of course . . ." He let his voice trail off.

Trying to hide his impatience, and not succeeding especially well, Worf said, "Of course what?"

"Well . . . as long as you're here," said Geordi, "the cadets are having the opportunity to experience, firsthand, close up, what a member of the proud Klingon race is like. You're breaking a lot of ice just by being here. If you can make them realize that Klingons are not the enemy, then you're doing a tremendous service to Klingons everywhere. How?" he said, anticipating Worf's question. "Because once your classmates graduate, they're going to be out on ships, exploring the galaxy. And, sooner or later, they'll run into Klingons.

"Now, do you want to run the risk of their giving whatever Klingons they encounter a tough time because maybe they're carrying all their old fears with them? Or do you want them, through their exposure to you over the next few years, to overcome their prejudices toward Klingons? And, as a result, be that much more likely to treat Klingons with the respect, dignity, and honor that they so richly deserve?"

"That is not fair," Worf said, starting to feel a little angry. "You cannot put all on me the notion that my being here in the Academy is going to have significant impact on the future dealings with other Klingons."

"I didn't intend to put anything on you," Geordi replied easily. "All I'm doing is pointing out the likely way that things are going to occur. It strikes me that it would be the honorable thing for you to stay here and try to make life better for the Klingon race. But that's not my decision, is it?"

Worf scowled, more darkly than he had in some time. "And to leave would be dishonorable, is that it?"

"You said that, not me. You just do what you feel you

have to do. Nowhere is it written that you have to make *me* happy."

Worf was silent for a moment . . . and then sighed very, very loudly.

At that, Geordi smiled. "Look, Mr. Worf, you're talking to the one other guy at the Academy who really, truly knows what it's like to feel separate from the rest of the world. You and I . . . we're pretty much alike. We both see things in ways that the rest of the people around us don't. You view them through the eyes of a Klingon born to respect honor and strength and a variety of other virtues. And I view the world, well, my way. It's lonely as anything. But it doesn't have to be that way. Not if you're willing to let people in . . . or let yourself out."

Worf nodded. At that, Geordi clapped him on the back. Then, as an afterthought, he added, "Are you going on the Prometheus Run?"

Worf looked up in confusion. "The what?"

"Routine stuff," said Geordi. "Prometheus is the artificial satellite at the outer end of the solar rim, the one that serves as a first-alert station in case of attack. It's all automated, but Starfleet likes to send a group of cadets out there once a year to run various routine checks. Upperclassmen always pick the away team. I know a guy on the committee. I could recommend you for it. What's your specialty?"

"Majoring in security, minoring in operations," said Worf. Actually, he hadn't really decided his specialties yet. That simply sounded like a good combination.

"Okay. It's basic stuff, pretty much, but it's a chance to get out into space. And, after all, that's really what it's all about, isn't it?"

"Yes, sir," said Worf quickly.

"It's been a pleasure meeting you, Cadet Worf."

"The same to you, sir."

Worf stood there and watched Geordi La Forge head back into the Academy.

Of all the humans that Worf had ever encountered, he decided, at that very moment, that Ensign Geordi La Forge was probably among the most unique. He was almost sad about the fact that La Forge would be gone soon.

He wondered if he would ever see him again.

CHAPTER

10

A week later an early rising sun over San Francisco found a dozen cadets assembled at the shuttle pad for the Prometheus Run. Although it had been a few weeks since Worf had arrived on this very landing pad, to a certain extent it seemed as if it was just yesterday. It was difficult to believe that so much had happened to him in such a brief period of time. For that matter, it was hard for him to believe that he was still there.

He was annoyed that he had allowed himself to fall so thoroughly for what that ensign had been saying. La Forge had boxed Worf in—he could see that now—phrased things in such a way that he had absolutely no choice in the matter. He'd made him feel that if he walked out of the Academy now, he would be hurting the entire Klingon Empire!

So he was going to hang around. At least until they threw him out.

The air was a little nippy that morning, and a stiff breeze

was blowing in from the ocean. It filled the air with a nautical sense, and for a moment Worf felt a connection with explorers from centuries ago. Back when they braved—not the stars in sky-spanning metal ships—but the oceans, in vessels made of creaking wood, held together with ancient devices called "nails."

What kind of men must they have been, those adventurers? Although there was so much about the mysteries of space that remained unknown, still, there was much of which they were already quite aware. But what of those first explorers, who grew up in a society that taught them that the world was flat, that dragons lived at the edges prepared to devour any unwary explorer who dared trespass. . . .

What must they have been like, those explorers?

"Insane."

He turned as he heard the comments from other students who were now gathering around the shuttle. It was Briggs who had been speaking, muttering to himself, "It's insane to have us up and about at this hour."

Worf was pleased to see the other members of his study group among the cadets who were embarking on the mission. It wasn't particularly surprising—the members of this crew were chosen from the higher grade achievers in the Academy. The study group, working as smoothly and efficiently as Simon had planned, had easily fallen into that rank. Worf might have had his difficulties when it came to socializing. But as far as academics was concerned, he didn't have to hang his head in shame.

There was Soleta, who would probably look self-possessed and prepared even in the middle of the night. Tania Tobias was rubbing the sleep out of her eyes, but otherwise seemed fairly prepared for the day's activities.

Mark McHenry was distracted, as always. Worf doubted that Mark had any problem with the early hour. He had once mentioned that he rarely slept, because he was always finding more interesting things to do. When asked about such biological needs as the dream sleep that was required for the psychological health of a human being, Mark had simply replied, "Oh, I do that while I'm awake." No one had the nerve to pursue the matter further.

For that matter, no one doubted him.

Zak Kebron was up and around. The Brikar had been snoring soundly that morning when Worf got up. Deep down, Worf had hoped that Zak would sleep right through the intended lift-off of the mission. He should have known that that was too much to hope for.

When the roster for the Prometheus Run had been posted earlier that week, Worf had almost expected a wave of protest when it was noted that his name was up there. Such did not occur, however. Starfleet cadets, it appeared, were made of stronger stuff than that. The extra work from Professor Lupisky had probably stifled most thoughts of rebellion.

But neither, however, were they going to go to any effort to make him feel welcome. When Worf had returned to his quarters after his talk with Geordi La Forge, Zak had been seated at his desk, studying, and barely glanced up upon Worf's entrance. "Oh. Still here?" he had asked. He did not seem angry or frustrated or glad or anything. It was simply an acknowledgment of the continued state of Worf's presence.

And that was very much what Worf had gotten from a number of other students over the next few days. An air of "Oh. Still here?" No one was going to raise a fist to him, but neither was anyone going to lend him a hand.

There were other cadets here, as well, talking animatedly with one another. They were bustling with varying degrees of excitement over their first mission, routine though it might be.

And there was Simon.

Worf stared at him.

He had not seen Simon for some days now. Simon had been skipping their customary meals together, saying he preferred to eat in his room, or not at all. Worf knew he had been burying himself in work, spending many additional hours going over and over various texts. Driven, Worf was sure, by the insatiable need to succeed beyond anyone's reasonable expectations. He'd even missed a couple of study groups, pleading exhaustion and stating that he was probably coming down with something.

Worf had been a bit concerned, at first. But he knew Simon was always going to be the type of person who was driven to produce beyond anything that anyone could rationally expect. That was part of what made Simon the born leader that he was, Worf had thought.

Still . . . not having seen Simon for a while, Worf felt some small measure of concern upon running into him now. He did not seem quite as robust as he usually did. His eyes had a slightly hollow look, as if he hadn't been sleeping particularly well as of late. He had definitely lost weight—nothing that made him look unhealthy, but enough to catch Worf's attention.

"Simon," he said in a low voice, "are you all right?"

Simon smiled gamely. "You know me," he said. "I'm not at my best early in the morning."

Worf certainly did know him. And he knew that Simon was perfectly tip-top early in the morning. All the time that they'd lived on the farm on Gault, early rising had been the norm.

Before he could inquire further, however, there was a brisk clapping of hands and a voice called out, "All right, cadets! On board!"

The shuttlecraft was sitting there, covered with a fine morning dew. The loading door had opened up, and from it emerged the self-defense teacher, Commander Clark. He clapped his hands together briskly and said, "You're not accomplishing anything just by standing around here. Let's do it!"

Immediately the cadets clambered on board. They were full of enthusiasm and excitement. This was the sort of thing they'd been training for.

Worf sat next to a window, keeping the seat next to him open for Simon. But to his surprise, his brother sat in the next row up, also next to the window. He leaned against it, staring out, and for just the briefest of moments Worf thought he saw an expression of bleak helplessness on Simon's face. But then it vanished as quickly as it had been there, and Worf told himself that he'd imagined it.

Tania leaned over to Worf and said, "Anyone sitting here?" She pointed to the empty aisle seat next to him.

Worf stared at the seat. "If they are, they are very well camouflaged," he replied.

Tania laughed and dropped into the seat next to Worf. "How about that," she said. "Worf actually made a joke."

"A joke?" he said. "Oh. I was serious, actually."

She sighed. "You're always serious. What makes a Klingon laugh?"

"Human beings in pain."

She stared at him and paled slightly.

"That was a joke," he told her. "Was it a good one?"

"Not particularly, no."

"Oh." He looked a little crestfallen. "I was attempting 'dark irony.' I did not succeed?"

"Keep working on it."

He sighed. "That's what my parents tell me. The human notion of humor is a very curious thing."

"That's for sure," she admitted.

Clark was seated in the pilot's seat. He swiveled in his seat and called back to the cadets, "Everyone strap in. We have a schedule to keep, so we're going to be lifting off fast."

They did so. As Worf snapped the buckle in tight, he noticed that Mark McHenry was sitting across the aisle. He wore an expression of such unbridled excitement that Worf was moved to ask, "What is the matter?"

Mark replied, "I just can't believe it, that's all. This is my first time going into deep space."

Tania and Worf stared at him incredulously. "Your *first time?*" Tania asked. "You've never gone far off planet before? Even on a family vacation or some such?"

He shook his head. "My schooling was entirely on Earth. And as for vacations, my father always said, 'Why go to all the trouble and expense of leaving Earth, when there are holoparlors for a fraction of the cost and aggravation?' Which, I guess, was true enough. Still . . ."

Worf shook his head. "It sounds very limiting to me."

"Me, too," Mark said confidentially, as if afraid that somehow his father—wherever he might be—might hear him. "Then again, my father always said I had way too much space between my ears anyway. I don't know what he meant by that. Do you?"

Worf and Tania exchanged a look. "No," they said together.

The engines of the shuttlecraft roared, and faster than Mark would have believed, the craft lifted off the pad. It hurtled skyward.

From where they were sitting, they could see through the portals the ground dwindling below them. Large puffy clouds floated in front of them. And then, in the blink of an eye, they were through the clouds and out of the atmosphere, where the blackness of space enveloped them.

"The stars," breathed Tania, amazed. "Look at them."

"What about them?" asked Worf.

"I'm always surprised that they're not twinkling."

"Of course not," Worf said reasonably. " 'Twinkling' is caused by the distortion of the starlight as it passes through the planetary atmosphere. Since—"

"Worf?"

"Yes, Tania?"

"Be quiet." She was busy gazing in wonderment. "Just be quiet."

They hurtled through space. The cadets continued to talk, but there was none of the loose bantering that had marked their earlier conversations. Instead their voices were low, and even a little unsure.

"Nervous, Worf?"

The question came from Zak Kebron, who was seated

behind Worf. Worf was surprised. He couldn't remember the last time that Zak had addressed him in a manner that was anything other than deliberately irritating.

"No. Should I be?"

"Well," Zak said easily, "here we are, out in space, heading toward the Prometheus satellite. Should be a standard mission, but you never know. This is the exact kind of situation they're always telling us about at the Academy . . . where all of us have to depend on one another. Aren't you the least bit nervous about your well-being depending upon a bunch of non-Klingons?"

Worf was about to reply, but abruptly Simon spun in his chair, propping himself up on one knee and turning to look over Worf in Zak's direction. And when he spoke, his voice was unexpectedly brittle and harsh.

"Cut it out, Kebron!" he almost snarled. "You have been on him since the day he got here, and it's *enough!* He's doing his best. We're all doing our best! And if that's not good enough for you, then you can—"

"I can what?" asked Zak calmly.

Commander Clark half-turned in his seat. "That's enough, back there! If you're interested in conducting yourselves in a civil manner, that's fine. If you're going to bicker, kindly keep it to yourselves. Understood?"

There were murmurs of "Yes, sir," and the shuttle lapsed into silence.

Worf leaned forward and whispered, "Simon, you did not have to—"

"Just enjoy the view, Worf," Simon replied, sounding old and tired.

Worf and Tania glanced at each other but said nothing.

The rest of the trip was fairly uneventful. At last Clark called out, "All right, cadets. Prepare for arrival."

They all strained their eyes, seeing nothing at first. But then, finally, they spotted the station. It appeared small at first, but grew with amazing speed. It gave them a real feeling for just how fast they were traveling, that something could seem so far away and be upon them so soon.

As if reading their minds, Clark commented, "In the early days of space travel a manned journey like this one would have been impossible due to fuel considerations. And even if they somehow had enough fuel, it would have taken months for them to cover the distance that we have in under an hour. Count yourselves lucky that you were born when you were. Because if you hadn't been—"

"Then my mother might still be pregnant with me," Mark offered, deadpan. "Eighteen years. Wow. That'd be a record, I think."

As was always the case with Mark, it was impossible to tell whether he was kidding or not. So no one tried.

Ahead of them hung Prometheus Station. It was old by any standard, having been there for decades. A living relic of the earliest days of the Federation. Back then the coming together of different civilizations seemed far more a matter of mutual protection from hostility than the forum for informed, intelligent, and nonbelligerent interaction that it had evolved into.

Completely automated, the Prometheus Station defense system and detection devices had really become outmoded. If it had been decommissioned and broken down for scrap, the odds were that it would have made no difference to Earth security. Not with the long-range sensor capabilities that Earth itself now possessed. But Prometheus was regarded as something of a historical landmark. And so it was maintained—kept up as a link with the rugged beginnings of the United Federation of Planets.

Prometheus Station was shaped like a giant top, with a large spiral encircling it that served as energy conduits. The shuttlecraft angled toward it, and Clark punched an entry code into the communications grid. Prometheus sat there for a moment, as if digesting this unexpected morsel of information. Then the ponderous shuttle bay door at the top opened. It seemed to take forever to do so—yet another indicator of the age of the station. Eventually it did open fully, and Clark guided the shuttle in with practiced ease.

The shuttle bay was so ancient that it did not have the forcefield that maintained an atmosphere while the doors were open. The cadets had to sit in the shuttle until the doors cycled shut and the atmospheric balance was restored once more. Then Clark got up to face them.

"You all have your assigned duties," he said. "Thorough check of all maintenance systems. Weapons systems. Detections systems. This station has six levels, and there are twelve of you. Simple math will tell you that you should be able to go through this in record time. Check for any current systems malfunctions and, more important, locate any lapses that could possibly lead to problems down the road. I want detailed reports of everything that you find. I will be stationed at the command core if there is any problem. Are your communications links on line?"

They each tapped the insignia communicator badge that had been issued them for the mission. Each heard a confirming *beep* upon touching it, and they all nodded affirmation.

"Excellent. All right, cadets. You received your assignments before we left Earth. Carry them out."

The exit door hissed open, and one by one the cadets filed out into the great shuttle bay of Prometheus Station.

CHAPTER

11

Worf checked the neutron flow along the graviton field and nodded in approval. On the one hand, this was a fairly boring procedure. On the other hand, at least it was going smoothly. If there had been a variation in the field of even one percentage point from the norm, then Worf might have had to spend hours trying to track down the source.

But the measurements were precisely where they were supposed to be.

Worf slid the wall panel shut and turned as Soleta came over to him. "All is well?" he asked.

She nodded. "The coils are sound. Structural integrity is still solid. I have not found anything to indicate any potential breakdowns in the station's efficiency or long-term—"

"Worf."

It was Simon's voice. Worf looked around, momentarily confused, and then he realized that his brother's voice was coming over the communications link.

Simon had been assigned to inspect the long-range monitor redundancies on Level 1. Worf tapped the comm link in response. "Yes, Simon."

"Worf, get up here. I want your opinion on something . . . fast."

Worf and Soleta glanced at each other. "If there is a problem—" began Worf.

"I'm not sure. I want someone double-checking these readings. Worf, I'm not kidding. Get up here."

"I will bring Soleta," said Worf.

"Fine, fine. Just move."

Without further discussion, Worf and Soleta ran down the corridor. They took the turbolift up three levels and emerged onto Level 1. Simon was standing there waiting for them.

"Come on," he said.

They hurried after him and arrived at the detection center to discover Zak Kebron standing there, going over some instrumentation. He looked up at the others.

"Where did you disappear to?" demanded Zak of Simon.

Simon didn't bother to answer him but instead turned to Worf and Soleta. "Check over subroutine system A, long range. Tell me what you see."

"I'll tell you what *I* see—" began Zak.

Worf cut him off, stepping up to the control panel. "No one asked you," he snapped. Soleta stood next to him, watching as his large hands moved quickly over the display. Worf's face creased in a frown.

"There is a blip," Worf said finally. "Some sort of electron flux. . . ."

"An intruder?" Soleta asked.

Worf shook is head. "It is not being picked up on any of the primary detectors."

"Do we tell Clark?" said Simon.

"Tell him what?" snarled Zak. "There can't be an intruder. If there were, the primary detection fields would have reported it. This place would be ringing with enough alarms to be heard halfway to Argelius. There can't be an intruder that's only being picked up by a third-level redundancy." He paused. "Maybe it's a spatial distortion flux."

"Get McHenry up here," said Worf. "No one knows spatial distortions like he does."

"The man *is* a spatial distortion," sniffed Zak.

"Right. Right. McHenry." Simon had sounded momentarily confused, as if he hadn't quite connected with the situation yet. He tapped his comm badge. "McHenry."

No answer.

"McHenry," he said again.

Still no answer.

The others looked worriedly at each other. "Mark, where the blazes are you?" snapped Simon.

"Right here."

They jumped as they turned. Mark McHenry was standing directly behind them, as if he'd materialized out of thin air.

"I was in between this level and the next one, climbing through a Jeffries tube," said Mark. "When you called, I just climbed the rest of the way up."

"We're picking up something on long-range scanners, but only through a third-level check system. Primary scanners aren't picking up anything. We think maybe it's being fooled by a spatial distortion flux."

"Either that, or maybe it's broken," offered Mark.

"We've run a primary check," said Soleta. "The system reads normal."

Mark shrugged. "Maybe what's broken is the check systems."

"Maybe we should get Tania up here," said Simon. "She's the engineering expert. . . ."

"Why don't we just have everybody up here," said Zak with a snort, "and make a party out of it?"

"No, it's okay," said Mark. He moved to a console. "I got a knack for this kind of stuff. This is the primary detection station, right?"

"Yeah. Right," said Simon.

"And if we were really in danger, there'd be alarms, right?"

"Right," Worf said. He was starting to get impatient.

"But since we're not," Mark continued, as if striving mightily to understand, "it means either that there's no danger . . . or else this thing here is broken."

"Right," Soleta now said. Even the Vulcan girl seemed a bit put off by Mark's denseness.

"Hmmm." Mark studied the console carefully, looking under it and around it.

"This is a waste of time," muttered Zak.

And then slowly, carefully, Mark drew back a hand, curled his fingers under . . .

And punched the console.

Immediately a massive thumping alarm went off that sounded throughout the station. The cadets looked at one another in momentary confusion—all except Mark McHenry, who was remarkably calm.

"Fixed it," said Mark.

Commander Clark's voice crackled over all of their comm badges at the same time. "What the devil's going on up there?" he demanded from the command core that ran down the middle of the station.

Instrumentation was flashing all around them. Readings were flooding in from every sensor device on board the station.

Worf waited a moment for Simon to respond. He was the one who had been assigned command of this particular level. Consequently, it was his responsibility to reply to Clark.

But Simon just stood there, all the color draining from his face.

"Commander, this is Worf!" the Klingon said quickly. "Instrumentation indicates we have a Level-One intrusion. A ship classified as belonging to a hostile species is within our defense perimeter!"

"Identify!" said Clark.

Soleta was already on it. She studied the readings and called out, "Configuration indicates a Romulan vessel, closing fast."

"I'm alerting Starfleet," said Clark. "Keep feeding me readings. Clark to Level Five. Prepare defensive weaponry—"

"Maybe they're after Worf," Zak said darkly. "They found out they missed one on Khitomer. . . ."

Worf's head snapped around. "How do you know about Khitomer?" he demanded.

Zak looked away, not responding.

"They're not cloaked!" yelled Mark. All of the vague mannerisms had vanished as the emergency had presented itself. "Why aren't they cloaked?"

"Logically," said Soleta with amazing calm, "they decloak when they are preparing to—"

Prometheus Station rocked around them, knocking all of them off their feet. Worf crashed to the ground, Soleta tumbling down atop him. Over the explosions and the shouts, they heard Clark yelling over the comm units. Telling them not to panic, telling them to do their jobs. . . .

On Level 5 Briggs and Tania had fired up the defensive array. They'd brought the shields on line and were charging up the phaser battery. But Briggs was fighting down panic. "Look at this stuff," he was growling. "This stuff is ancient! We'd have better luck crawling outside and throwing bricks at them. . . ."

Then the Romulan warbird fired. They staggered. Tania grabbed the underside of a console and barely managed to keep her footing, but Briggs went down. "Shields at seventy-three percent!" she shouted.

"Fire!" Clark was bellowing over their comm links. "Fire!"

Briggs had struck his head when he fell. Now he lay on the floor, unconscious. Fighting down the bleak thought of *First mission in space and now I'm going to die here,* Tania scanned the weapons array. For a fleeting moment she thought she had the warbird targeted, and then she lost it. But she had to make an immediate response, or they were all dead.

She hit the firing buttons without a target lock, taking her best guess and tossing off a quick prayer. The phasers blasted out from Prometheus. Tania hoped that the instruments would tell her that the attacker was little more than floating shards of metal.

But instead, her reply was to feel the space station shudder once more under the impact of the Romulan plasma cannons. Her horrified gaze rested upon the latest readouts: The shield strength was down to twenty-three percent. Even modern deflectors couldn't take a pounding forever, and the shields of Prometheus were far from the latest technology.

She hit her comm link. "Tobias to everyone!" she called out. "Shields failing. One or two more hits, and they'll collapse! I'm trying to return fire, but I'm all alone down here!"

Then they were hit again . . . and that was when she heard the scream.

They all heard it through their open comm links—the scream that echoed from the command core.

It was Clark's voice. And they also heard over their comm links the sound of something crashing down, cutting off the scream before it had quite reached full voice.

On Level 1 the cadets looked at one another, ashen. They all knew what that sound meant.

"Clark's dead," whispered Simon.

And then the station was hit again. Consoles overloaded and blew out, and huge chunks of the ceiling began to rain down. Worf yanked Soleta out of the way just in time as debris crashed down on the spot where she'd been standing.

On their comm links they heard Tania's alarmed shriek. "Shields failing! Phaser batteries overheating!"

"Clark's dead," Simon was saying again. There was no color in his face at all. "He's dead! *We're all dead!*"

The floor started to buckle under them. *"Come on!"* shouted Worf, and he charged for the door.

It didn't open. The systems were down.

Simon was hysterical. Tears rolled down his face, and he was screaming, *"We're trapped! We're trapped!"*

"Shut up!" shouted Mark.

"Zak! *Now!*" Worf called to the Brikar, who immediately understood. He ran full tilt, slamming his massive, rock-hard shoulder into the door. The impact was enough to bend it ever so slightly, and Worf was able to work his fingers into the space. He grunted, pulling with all his strength, and now Zak joined him. For seconds that seemed an eternity, nothing happened. Then all at once the door ripped right out of the frame.

"Go! Everybody out!" shouted Worf. All around them the shattered machinery was starting to flare up, fire eating away at the ancient paneling.

Simon didn't move. "There's nowhere to go," he was sobbing. "There's nowhere to go. . . ."

Worf grabbed Simon by the shoulders. "We are still alive!" he grated. "We quit when we are dead! Not before!"

The other cadets were already out, and Worf practically lifted Simon off his feet and hurled him out of the room. Worf leapt out after him, and then the entire ceiling caved in.

The cadets charged down the hallway. "Where are we going?" shouted Mark.

"Tobias to anyone. Please respond." Tania's voice crackled over their comm links.

"All cadets: Meet us in the shuttle bay!" called Worf. "It is our only chance!"

The doors to the turbolift shaft hung open, with no turbolift in sight. Smoke was pouring out of it. The cadets, with Zak in the lead, skidded to a halt in front of it.

"The emergency walkways!" called Worf. "If we can get down to—"

Prometheus Station was hit again, and the wall at the far end of the corridor blew out. The station angled sharply, sending the cadets tumbling. . . .

And Zak Kebron, knocked off his feet, fell straight into the open turboshaft.

He reached out desperately, his arms flapping about. At the last second his three fingers curled around the lip of the entrance. He dangled there by one hand, smoke billowing around him. Even through his thick skin, he felt the heat searing him. His small eyes watered. Five levels below him an inferno was raging at the bottom of the shaft.

The metal he was clutching abruptly bent and started to break, and then a firm hand snagged around his wrist.

"I have you!" Worf shouted down to him. He was holding on to Zak with one hand; with the other he was clutching the doorframe. Soleta was on her stomach, reaching down and shouting, "Your other hand! Give me your other hand!"

Without thinking, Zak reached up and grabbed Soleta's outstretched arm. It was only then that a flash of alarm went through his mind. What if he wound up dragging them both down into the shaft with him? But the Vulcan science technician also had the formidable strength of a young Klingon, and she absorbed the pull on her arms without the slightest flinch.

Zak's feet pinwheeled desperately, and he managed to find enough of a toehold to help propel himself upward.

In a second Worf and Soleta had pulled Kebron up and to safety.

There was no time for conversation. "Quickly!" said Worf. "We must get to the—"

It was too late.

They heard a sound like a death knell—the world being ripped apart around them. Worf saw Simon collapse, sobbing and clutching at his knees, pulling into a fetal position. Then, in a searing flash of light and blast of deafening sound, the Prometheus Station was swallowed in the fire that its mythological namesake had brought to mankind.

Worf lost his footing . . . not surprising, because abruptly the floor was gone. The rending of metal and the death screams of the satellite itself drowned out everything else. Flame leapt up all around them, blocking every possible escape.

And then, above the ear-shattering cacophony, Worf called out final words of defiance.

"I go to join my Klingon parents!" he shouted. *"Cadets . . . I salute you! It is a good day to die!"*

And then the heat was gone, as was the station . . . and the cadets were hurled into the vast, airless, freezing vacuum of space.

And as they floated helplessly, waiting for death to claim them, they saw, in the cold depths, Commander Clark. . . .

And he was standing perfectly still.

And smiling.

And waving.

CHAPTER

12

"Computer . . . end program."

Three words, spoken, that they should not have been able to hear.

But there were the words, spoken by presumed-dead Commander Clark, in his calm, no-nonsense voice.

And space, and the shattered remains of the ill-fated Prometheus Station, all vanished.

The cadets, all twelve of them, found themselves lying on a floor. The room they were in was vast, and solid black, with a crisscrossing yellow grid all around.

The only solid object there, aside from themselves, was the shuttlecraft they had traveled in to . . .

To . . .

"Where are we?" asked Worf in confusion.

But it was Mark McHenry who understood immediately. "A holoparlor," he said in amazement. "We're . . . we're in a holoparlor. On—"

"Earth," Clark finished for him. He slowly surveyed

the amazed stares of the cadets. "You never left Earth. The shuttle was specially designed for holoillusions in the windows to simulate departure. The top of this training center is a retractable roof. Actually we landed in this holodeck . . . and have been here the entire time."

"Training center?" said Worf.

"Training center," confirmed Clark. "Learning the theories of how to deal with difficult—even terminal—situations is all well and good. But there's nothing like solid, practical experience."

Simon had gotten to his feet. His breath sounded ragged in his chest. "Ex—experience?"

"Of course," said Clark. "Throughout your career, you—"

"Experience!" With a roar Simon lunged at Clark.

Clark took a surprised step back, and Simon would have been at his throat if Worf hadn't caught him and held him back. "Simon, calm down!" he said. "It was a test! We are all right!"

Slowly Simon brought himself under control. Gradually he looked around and saw the eyes of the other cadets upon him.

He straightened up, smoothed out his jacket. And then he said, "Computer . . . exit."

A door appeared at one end of the room.

Without a word, Simon left.

"Do not go," Worf said. "Please."

Simon was packing the last of his things. He stood there in civilian clothes, his cadet uniforms hanging neatly in the closet. He glanced up at Worf.

And smiled. For the first time in a long time, he smiled. The genuine, warm Simon smile of old.

"It's done, Worf," he said. "I'm done."

"We can speak to someone," Worf told him. "So you did poorly this time. You can still—"

"Worf, don't you understand? Don't you get it yet? This is . . . this is a relief. I'm not cut out for Starfleet. I know that now."

"Nonsense," Worf said fiercely. "You can do whatever you want to do."

"Perhaps. But I *don't* want to do this."

He sat on the edge of his bed a moment, staring at his packed bag. "Years of growing up with Father's stories of Starfleet, and his expectations, and . . . well, I just *assumed* that this was what I wanted. But it's not. I was overwhelmed by the studies, the demands, the life-and-death high-risk gambles involved with being in Starfleet. I mean, come on, Worf. You saw how I was getting. You saw how I was struggling. I kept waiting for you to say something, but you didn't. Why?"

Worf gestured helplessly. "I—I thought you were faking it. Acting as if you were having a difficult time in order to make me feel better about myself. So I would not feel inferior to you."

At that, Simon laughed. He got up, walked across the room, and faced his brother. "You have no reason to feel inferior to anybody. Ever. You understand that? And you're going to stay here, and you're going to succeed, and you're going to have an incredible career, Worf. You understand me?"

Worf nodded.

"I'm going to hug you," Simon announced.

Worf sighed. "I was afraid of that."

Simon threw his arms around his brother and hugged him . . . very briefly. He didn't want to push Worf's tolerance further than necessary. He stepped back and said, "Make us proud."

"Do you have any doubt that I will?" asked Worf.

Simon picked up his bag, walked to the door, and turned to face Worf.

"None," he replied.

And then he was gone.

Zak Kebron was lying on his bunk, reading, when Worf walked in. He stepped carefully, so as not to tread on the other side of the room, and flopped down in his favorite study chair.

"You know," said Worf, "now that Simon is gone, McHenry could use a roommate. Perhaps if we spoke to Admiral Fincher . . ."

"We could convince her to separate us? Put one of us in with McHenry, and end this . . . mutual punishment?"

Worf nodded.

Zak didn't say anything for a time.

"Humans don't understand us," he said finally.

"I agree," said Worf.

"For example," continued Zak, "a human might think that your attempt to save my life when we thought we were on the exploding space station—a *human*, mind you—might think that your actions would make me think better of you. Would make me think that you were capable, and trustworthy, and loyal to the idea of Starfleet above all else."

"True," said Worf gravely. "But humans would not understand the famous Brikarian stubbornness."

"Equal only," Zak observed, "to the notorious Klingon stubbornness."

"We agree again," said Worf.

They were silent once more for a time.

"There's no point going to Fincher," Zak said at last. "She'd just insist we should stay together, in the vain *human* hope that we'd grow to respect, and maybe even— heaven forbid—like each other."

"Ridiculous."

"Absurd."

"Ludicrous. Still"—Worf sighed—"you are most likely correct. It would appear that we are stuck with each other."

"Indeed."

Worf picked up his padd and began to study the next day's lessons. Then he glanced over at the enforced border that ran down the middle of the room.

"You know," he said slowly, "that line is very unsightly."

Zak barely afforded it a glance. "Oh. That thing. I'd all but forgotten it was there. Get it cleaned off the floor, would you?"

"Why me?"

"*You* found it unsightly."

"Yes, but *you* put it there."

"Oh, whatever," said Zak impatiently. "We'll discuss it later . . . when we have less important things to do."

"Right," said Worf.

Zak looked at him. "You always have to have the last word, don't you?"

Worf looked back. "Yes."

Zak Kebron made a noise that sounded very much like a Brikar equivalent of a snicker, and then went back to his reading.

About the Author

PETER DAVID is a prolific author, having written in the past several years nearly two dozen novels and hundreds of comic books, including issues of such titles as *The Incredible Hulk, Spiderman, Star Trek, X-Factor, The Atlantis Chronicles, Wolverine,* and *The Phantom.* He has written several popular *Star Trek: The Next Generation* novels, including *Imzadi, Strike Zone, A Rock and a Hard Place, Vendetta,* and *Q-in-Law*—the latter three spending a combined three months on *The New York Times* bestsellers list. His other *Star Trek* novels include *The Rift* and *Star Trek: Deep Space Nine: The Siege.*

His other novels include *Knight Life* (a satirical fantasy in which King Arthur returns to contemporary New York and runs for mayor), *Howling Mad* (a send-up of the werewolf legend), the *Psi-Man* and *Photon* adventure series, and novelizations of "The Return of the Swamp Thing" and "The Rocketeer." He also writes a weekly column, "But I Digress . . ." for *The Comic Buyer's Guide.*

Peter is a longtime New York resident, with his wife of fifteen years, Myra, (whom he met at a Star Trek convention) and their three children: Shana, Guinevere, and Ariel.